Ryan GALLAGHER

ANNIE JOCOBY

VINCI BOOKS

Vinci Books

vinci-books.com

Published by Vinci Books Ltd in 2025

1

The publisher and the author have made every effort to obtain permissions
for any third party material used in this book and to comply with copyright
law. Any queries in this respect should be brought to the attention of the
publisher and any omissions will be corrected in future editions.
A CIP catalogue record for this book is available from the British Library.
Paperback ISBN: 9781036707293
The EU GPSR authorised representative is Logos Europe, 9 rue Nicolas
Poussion, 17000 La Rochelle, France contact@logoseurope.eu

By Annie Jocoby

Illusions

Beautiful Illusions
Deeper Illusions
End of Illusions

Chapter One

RYAN

"I'm pregnant," Alexis said to me as we sat on the back patio of my new place in Kansas City. I had just moved here after a rather trying few years in college. I wasn't on drugs anymore, having quit several year before. At that time, I was finally ready for drug sobriety. I had just had enough. It was a mental thing, where a switch was finally flipped, and I knew that my days of puking, shaking, and feeling that I needed another fix constantly were too much.

"I'm sorry?" I said to her. "Come again?"

"I'm pregnant," she said. "You heard me right."

I just sat there, dumbly. I had no idea how to react to this news. To say that I was a little taken aback would be understating the matter. "Okay," I said. "I'm not even sure how this happened. I thought we were being careful."

"I thought so, too," she said, but she didn't meet my eyes. "Well, I might have forgotten to take a pill or two along the way. I didn't think that it would matter, though."

I took a deep breath. It was just starting to sink in.

Alexis was pregnant. Pregnant. She and I weren't even together. We had just slept together the one time. We had broken up, again, for the last time, after the disastrous Hamptons summer. Well, the summer started fine, and fun, and everything was all good. Then she and Nick started screwing around behind my back, which turned out to be totally uncool and against the ground rules that we had set out for each other when the summer began. We broke up after that, of course, and that break-up I thought would be our last.

Now this. I should have listened to my gut, which was screaming at me to leave well enough alone where Alexis was concerned. I didn't want to be with her anymore. I was ready to move on from the toxicity that always plagued our relationship from the very start. I was ready to leave all that behind. I was ready to finally find the relationship I deserved. One that wasn't based upon a mutual love of drugs and sex, with a healthy dose of loathing for one another.

It now seemed that my hope to get away from her wouldn't exactly be in the cards just yet. "Okay. Well, the obvious question is whether it's mine."

Her eyes were downcast. "I know. I really have no idea if it is. That's why I'd like for us to get an *in utero* DNA test so we can figure things out. No purpose in putting you through this if it's not even yours."

I sighed. Boy, this was something that surprised me. I thought about Michael Corleone, lamenting about being pulled back in, just when he thought he was out. Just when I thought I was going to leave all of that bullshit that came with Alexis behind, this happens.

"Schedule the DNA test as soon as you can. I need to

know one way or another." I narrowed my eyes. "Alexis, you do know that Nick might be the father, don't you?"

"Of course," she said. "Of course, I know that. God forbid that's the case, though. I would imagine that would probably mean that you and he will never be able to repair your friendship."

I shook my head. Nick was my best friend, always. He saved my life so many goddamned times. Yet, we weren't on speaking terms because of what happened with him and Alexis. And if he happened to be the father of Alexis' baby...well, we would probably get past it. We got past a lot worse. But it would certainly be just one more thing that would come between us.

"Nick and I will be fine, eventually," I said. "Don't worry about us. If we can still be friends after that fight we had over my drug use, where I sent him to the hospital, we'll be friends through anything. But it will be weird, of course, if he's the father." I cleared my throat. "And who else might be?"

She shrugged. "It could be Seth. It could also be Peter. And, well, that's really all."

What a mess. "Who are these other two guys?"

She twirled her hair and didn't meet my eyes. "I met them at a bar a couple of weeks ago."

"Say no more," I said, shaking my head. "What are you going to do if the father is somebody else? Hell, what are you going to do if I'm the father?"

"What does that supposed to mean?" she asked me. "Are you implying I might get an abortion?"

"I'm not implying anything," I said. "But that's an option, of course, at least in Kansas."

"That's not an option," she said, her blue eyes flaring with indignation. "You know how I feel about that."

3

I did know how she felt about that. Alexis was a lot of things, but pro-choice wasn't one of them. No, that wasn't exactly correct – she felt strongly that women, in general, should have the choice. But she never felt that she, herself, would make such a choice.

"I understand," I said. "But that complicates things immensely, of course."

"Maybe, maybe not," she said, and then took a deep breath. "I've been hoping and praying you're the father. To tell you the truth, it would be an answer to my prayers, in general, about us."

"Meaning?"

"I want us to be together, Ryan, for real. No more games, no more lying, no more cheating. No more drug use. Just you and me and a new baby. I think that us having a baby would be the greatest thing to happen to us. It'll make us more solid and would really be the glue that will hold us together."

I got up out of my chair and paced around. "Alexis, I honestly don't think I know where I would be if you didn't come into my life when you did. If you didn't convince Nick to take me in when you did. But you're being naïve if you think that a baby, or anything else, is going to make us solid. We don't belong together, Alexis. We just don't."

Her blue eyes started to brim with tears. "What are you saying? If I have this baby, you're not going to be in the child's life? We're not going to be a family? You wouldn't do that to me, I know you wouldn't. Your family is broken. So is mine. I think you want to give this child a better chance than you and I have gotten, don't you?"

I sat back down and put my arm around her. "Of course I do. And if the child is mine, and that's a huge 'if,' but if this child is mine, then I'll step up to the plate."

"Really? By step up to the plate, you mean…"

Deep breath. "We'll get married. And hopefully stay married."

At that, she wrapped her arms around me and started bawling. "Oh, I was hoping you would say that to me. I was so scared that you would just abandon me. We can make this work, just wait and see. You and I can make it work."

I gently pushed her off of me. "We're getting ahead of ourselves. We have no idea if this baby is mine. I probably shouldn't have told you about us getting married until we figured that part out."

She nodded her head rapidly. "I know, I know, I know, Ryan. God, I hope it's yours. I love you so much. I know I don't always show it, but I do. More than you'll ever know."

Oh, this is just great. She was going on about how much she loved me, but I didn't feel the same for her anymore. Not that I ever did. Alexis was somebody I liked, very much, but I just didn't feel the overwhelming desire and passion for her that I wanted to feel.

I wondered if I ever would feel that way about another person.

Still, Alexis had some truly wonderful qualities. As long as she was faithfully taking her meds, she was a sweet person. It was when the meds stopped working, or she went off them - which she often did because she would start to feel better and would assume she didn't need them anymore – that the real trouble began.

I didn't tell her I loved her, even though she had just told me. "We'll cross that bridge when we come to it, Alexis, but you have to know one thing. And that is that I won't stay with you unless you agree to stay on your meds." I sighed. "Let's not even talk about this, Alexis. Let's talk about this when we find out who the father is. If I'm the dad, we'll get married, but you're going to have to agree to my terms."

I was going to have to draw up a list of terms for her. It was going to be a long list, but that would be the only way she and I could ever make it work.

Chapter Two

Alexis and I were waiting, nervously, to find out the results of the DNA test. The past few days had been pins and needles. I had no idea, really, what was going to happen if the child was mine. I know that I already was committed to marrying her, but, in my mind, I could think of no worse outcome than that. I would be there for her, that was for sure, but I couldn't help but think that I would feel trapped.

I would be trapped into a loveless marriage with her. And I would be trapped by the overall toxicity of how we were together. It didn't exactly seem fair that I would be resigned to such a life, but it wasn't like I wasn't to blame. I was, of course. I was the one who had sex with her without using a condom. I knew she probably was careless with her birth control, just because she was so goddamned careless about everything in her life.

I just had to go along, every day, as if there wasn't a Sword of Damocles hanging over my head. Which there was, of course. There was a huge sword over my head, and it was going to come down at any moment. Even if that

7

child wasn't mine, there would be problems. If it belonged to Nick, that would be an enormous problem. If it belonged to the other two random guys Alexis hooked up with, then there would be a problem, because Alexis had a major problem with spending. And who knew if either of those two random guys had enough money to pay child support.

Who knew if Alexis even had the means to contact either of them? That thought occurred to me, too. These were two random guys at a bar.

My suspicions were confirmed when I asked Alexis about them. "Alexis, suppose that neither Nick nor I are the father. Do you have a way to get ahold of those other two guys?"

Her eyes were downcast and she said nothing.

"Alexis, do you know their last names?"

She shrugged.

I shook my head. "Alexis, are you even sure their names are Peter and Seth?"

She shook her head.

Oh, what did it matter? Even if those were their first names, how would we even get in touch with either of them? I supposed that I could get on the Internet and look up the number for every Seth and Peter in the Kansas City area. Ha ha.

I took another deep breath. "Alexis. What do you know about these two men?"

"I don't know anything about them, okay?" she said to me, suddenly angry that I was questioning her too much. "I met them, I was drunk, so were they, they suggested I go home with them, and I agreed. I can barely remember what either of them looked like, let alone anything else about them. I don't think I could pick either of them out of a lineup at this point."

Great. This was just great.

At the same time, I knew this had to be a common problem. Alexis wasn't the only woman who got drunk at a bar and ended up knocked up because of it. Probably wouldn't be the last, either. I wondered what other women did when they were faced with just such a dilemma – getting pregnant by somebody whose last name was unknown.

Again, though, we would cross that bridge when we came to it.

"Sorry for pressing you too much, Alexis, but we have to face reality here. There's a good chance this child doesn't belong to me or Nick. There's a fifty-fifty chance of that, in fact. I just want you to be prepared for that, and we'll have to figure out how to tackle that problem if it crops up. That's all."

Her fingers were rapping on the table in front of her. She suddenly was in her pissed-off mood. That was the way she was. She could be as sweet as pie one second, but say the wrong thing, and she could be a raging beast. "What would you have me do, Ryan? I'm obviously not as together as you are. I can see you're judging me, which is really rich, coming from you. Really rich. What, you finally get off the drugs, and that gives you the right to judge me? What the fuck, Ryan?"

I made a face. "Who said anything about judging you? I'm just trying to get you to face facts here. And the facts are that-"

"That I'm a whore. I'm a whore, and I deserve to be saddled with a brat who has no idea who her father is. How can I afford to raise a child all on my own? You answer me that, Ryan."

"Alexis, quit putting words in my mouth. I never called you a whore. I never even implied it. And I don't judge you for not kicking drugs, either. I know you struggle with it and I know you're trying. You're doing a good job, aside from your occasional relapses. But that's neither here nor there. You have to be prepared to have a plan for if neither Nick nor I are the father of this baby. That's all."

She looked like she wanted to strangle me. "Oh, that's right. That's right. You're a man. Nothing like this can ever happen to you. Literally. You'll never have to raise a child on your own because you lost track of your fuck partners. So you can judge me all you want, but if you were in my shoes, you would be pretty goddamned panicked."

And there it was. Alexis was panicked. That was why she was lashing out at me. I needed to talk her off the ledge.

"Alexis," I said. "First off, all this talk might be idle. This baby might be mine, and I'll be there to help you take care of it. I have more than enough money to support a new baby and you as well. Think positively. Granted, there's only a one in four chance I'm the father, but those are pretty good odds. So, let's just focus on that right now, okay? Stop thinking the worst."

She looked calmer. "Well, you were the one who brought up the worst-case scenario to me. Are you trying to set me off?"

"No, I'm trying to get you prepared. But I can see that's the wrong approach to take, so I'm now saying that you need to not assume the worst, but assume the best."

The best for her, of course, would be if I were the father. That would be not the best for me, though. I wished I were the kind to cut and run, but I wasn't. I wasn't, and I was going to be a stand-up guy here, if the child was mine. Sacrifice my own happiness to ensure the baby has an intact family, lots of love, and lots of money.

ON THE FIFTH DAY after Alexis and I went in to do the DNA testing, we got the results. They came in the mail, and I went to the mailbox and nervously brought in the official-looking envelope.

"It's here," I said, seeing my hands were shaking.

She looked pale and terrified. "Don't open it yet. I'm not ready to see yet."

"Alexis, I have to open it," I said. "We have to know what's going to happen here."

"I know that," she said. "But I'm really scared. What if it isn't you?"

She was afraid it wasn't me.

I was afraid it was.

Both of us were nervous about getting the results, but we were nervous for directly opposite reasons.

"Alexis," I said. "I have to open the results. I have to know right now."

"Okay," she said. "Go ahead."

I took a deep breath and opened the envelope and read it.

With a sinking heart, I read the unborn child was mine.

Chapter Three

Okay, so the unborn child was mine.

Time for a prenup.

Alexis looked extremely happy. "Oh my God, it's my dream come true," she said to me. "We're finally going to be okay. We're going to be a family." She was beaming. "I've dreamed about this day, Ryan. The day when you and I would have something that brings us together and keeps us together. And we're going to get married."

She did a little dance around the room.

I groaned. This was the last thing I wanted, to tell the truth. I so wanted to find The One. The woman who made me weak in my knees. The woman for whom I would gladly walk through fire. Alexis certainly wasn't it.

But she was my future. She was my future, and I was going to have to deal with it, somehow, someway.

It was that day that I saw her. I was downtown that day, going to my lawyer's office. Sheldon was in a high-rise, and he was my lawyer for everything I did. He had written up my will, he had looked over my employment contract, and he was always doing various things for me. He even got me out of a few legal scrapes back in my drug days.

And now I was going to him to have him draw up a pre-nup.

I was talking on the phone to him, telling him I was running just a bit late, when a redheaded woman passed right by me on the street.

And there was something about her that made me lose my breath.

She was dressed in a too-tight blue suit with running shoes on her feet. I smiled, charmed that she apparently didn't care how goofy she looked. Alexis would never wear running shoes with her suits. She cared, far too much, what other people thought.

But as I watched this woman, I realized why she needed running shoes. Because she was literally running somewhere. She was out of breath, carrying a huge file in her hand, and huffing it up the street while frantically checking her watch. Something about her made me want to find a rickshaw and whisk her to wherever she wanted to go.

As I wordlessly watched her sprinting towards the court-house, I shook my head. What was it I felt when she brushed by me at top speed?

I shook my head. That certainly was weird.

But I found myself following her up the street. I had no idea why.

Because I was so much taller than she was, I was soon behind her, and I watched her as she got to the door of the courthouse and took off her running shoes and put on her heels. Something she was wearing set off the metal detector, and I saw her make a gesture in frustration. I went in behind her, and I saw her get stopped by another attorney, and gesture to him about her running late.

I was still trying to figure out what was going on in my head as I got on the elevator with her. I only knew that I had a sudden urge to get to know her. To ask her name and introduce myself.

But I couldn't do that, of course. I was going to be married soon. With a baby on the way.

So, I really couldn't understand why I was so drawn to this woman. I hadn't really had that reaction with anybody else in my entire life. I stood behind her on the elevator and inhaled her scent. It was some kind of floral perfume. She was breathing heavily, shaking her head, dancing from side to side nervously, and talking to herself.

"She's going to kill you," she said to herself. "She warned you about being late. Why are you such a procrastinator?"

I smiled and another attorney started to talk to her. "Where are you supposed to be?"

"In Ruben's court," she said. "You know how pissed she is when attorneys are late."

"Sometimes. Sometimes she'll murder you for being a second late. Sometimes she doesn't care. Let's hope you catch her on a good day."

"I'm never that lucky," she said. "Come on, you stupid elevator, come on." She was looking at the elevator lights, which were slowly, slowly climbing from one floor to the next. She addressed the other attorney. "Do you think this elevator is deliberately trying to get me into more trouble?"

The other attorney smiled and shook his head. "You got a client waiting for you?"

"No, thank God. It's just a status conference. Unfortunately, I don't think I'm ready for it, either. I'm kinda a hot mess today."

I stood behind her, thinking of something to say. Something that would not seem like I was prying into her business, but would, at the same time, make her look at me.

"No offense, but you're kind of a mess, in general," the other attorney said with a smile.

"Har har," she said. "Look who's talking."

The elevator got to her floor, and she rushed out.

I wanted to get off the elevator, too. I really did. But I knew it was pointless.

Of course it was pointless. What would be the point in introducing myself to this woman and getting to know her?

I was going to be married. In fact, that was the reason why I was downtown in the first place. To see my lawyer about a prenup.

As I rode the elevator back down, and got into the street, I thought about that woman. Who was she, and why did I feel like I had to follow her? Why did just being close to her send a jolt of electricity that I hadn't yet felt with any woman, least of all Alexis?

I shook my head, and tried to shake it off.

And I headed to Sheldon's office.

"SORRY I'M LATE," I said to Sheldon, as I entered his office. I didn't tell him why I was late. He would have thought that I was beyond bizarre if I told him I was late because of an encounter with a woman who I had never seen before, but who lit up my entire body like I had never before thought possible. Here I was asking him to draw up a prenup prior to my marriage with Alexis, and I was just on the street daydreaming about somebody else.

That mystery woman referred to herself as a hot mess. That was how I was feeling right at that moment.

"It's okay," he said. "I had a conference call before you came in, anyhow." He shook his head. "So, you're finally going to make Alexis an honest woman. I never thought I would see the day."

"Neither did I," I said honestly. "But she's pregnant, so…"

"Say no more," he said. "But that's really old-fashioned of you to marry her. And I wouldn't recommend it."

I knew he wouldn't recommend it. He knew me and he knew Alexis. He knew how volatile we had always been together. He knew everything – about the drug use, about how I was always bailing her out. About her cheating on me, which was why we usually ended up breaking up. He even knew about Alexis' affair with Nick at the Hamptons' house, and the fact that they recently slept together.

In other words, he knew how toxic Alexis and I were together.

"I understand," I said. "That's why this prenup has to be airtight. I don't anticipate Alexis and I staying together for a long period of time. I wish I could say differently, because there's going to be a child involved, but I can't. I have little hope that this is going to be a 'til death do us part' situation."

Sheldon chewed on a pencil. "Ryan, is there any way I can talk you out of this? I hate to see you marry somebody who you hate more than you love."

I looked out the window and thought about the mystery woman. How she made me feel, just when she passed by me. Just standing behind her on the elevator. It was a weird feeling for me, one that I hadn't ever experienced.

If I believed in that sort of thing, I would have thought

that seeing her was a sign. A sign that I wasn't supposed to be marrying Alexis, baby or no baby.

But I didn't believe in things like signs, so I shook it off. "Duly noted. You think this is a mistake. And I agree. I agree. But there's a baby on the way, and, well, I never really had a family. Except for Nick's family, and thank God for that. But it would have been nice, growing up as a young boy, to have had a stable unit."

Sheldon shook his head. "That's just it. You and Alexis probably won't be a stable unit. You might think that having a piece of paper might make the two of you actually like each other, but, trust me, I'm a divorce lawyer, too. I've been in the middle of some wars where the two people actually were in love when they got married. In your case, there isn't even that going in. And I've always been there when it all goes south. You and Alexis are probably going to go south rather quickly."

I sighed. I knew he was right, but I also knew what I had to do. "I know what you're saying, and you're saying it as a friend, not my lawyer. Because you know how much money I'm going to be paying you if Alexis and I don't last. You'll be making bank off me, so, by advising me not to marry Alexis, you're advising me against your own financial interests. So that does mean a lot to me. But I have to do this. I have to try."

He shook his head. "Okay, then, since you're dead set for this, I've drawn up a preliminary agreement for her to sign. This agreement assumes, of course, that everything you bring into the marriage is yours in the event the two of you divorce. That's not a problem, that's just law. But I need to protect these assets in the event they appreciate considerably over the years. And they will. Especially your Cézanne and your de Kooning."

I nodded. "Alright, let's take a look at those papers." Sheldon handed them to me and I examined them closely. Everything seemed to be airtight – Alexis wouldn't be entitled to much at all, relatively, if she and I got divorced. Which was probably a good thing, but, at the same time, I knew Alexis. I knew how she was. She was going to scream bloody murder when she saw this prenup.

But I still had the upper hand in these negotiations. I could just walk away and agree only to pay her child support. Alexis knew this. I wasn't emotionally invested in marrying her, not like she was emotionally invested in marrying me. And she had to know that, if she and I didn't get married, she would have a difficult time raising the child on her own.

So, yeah, I held all the cards. Let her scream bloody murder, I really didn't care.

"Looks good," I said. "Basically, if Alexis and I get divorced, she'll be leaving with little else but the clothes on her back, a child support order, and $10 million in cash. Of course, the child support order would be substantial, but I know Alexis. She'll blow through any money I give her like water."

"I'm glad you approve of this agreement," Sheldon said. "So, go and present it to her as soon as you can. I would imagine that she'll give it to her lawyer and the negotiations can begin."

I shrugged. "She and her lawyer can try to negotiate all they want. They're going to cave, because Alexis has no leverage here."

Sheldon and I talked for a few more minutes, and I left his office.

I decided to head to a bar in the Power and Light District to have a drink. My mind returned to the mystery woman who was running up the street. It was really the oddest thing. I had never turned my head that much for any woman in my life. She was just an ordinary woman. But her passing by me gave me such a powerful jolt of electricity....

I shook my head and ordered a scotch and water from the waitress. She brought it and I started drinking it and contemplating what was about to happen. I was going to be sucked in and I was going to be stuck. I wasn't the type that would cut and run when the going got rough, and I also wasn't the type who would ever be unfaithful.

On the bright side, there was going to be a baby. A new life. I really wanted, desperately wanted, to give this child the life I never had. Until Nick's family had taken me in, my life was filled with abuse and instability. I loved my mother, but she always had problems due to her mental illness. Even when I was a little boy, she would go catatonic and not speak to anybody for days. Other times, she would apparently hear voices, because she was speaking, but she was speaking to the air or the wall.

And my father...I tried not to think about him and what he did. He was abusive when I was very young. He beat me for the slightest things. And, in the dark recesses of my brain, I knew there was more that was associated with my dad. No clue, really, what that was. But I was pretty sure my father was responsible for screwing me up royally.

I had the chance to make things right for this child, and I was going to do it. I was going to give him or her every chance of really being happy. I was going to be the father that mine wasn't. And that really should be enough.

ALEXIS, OF COURSE, WAS NONE too happy to read the details of the prenup. In fact, she was outraged that there even *was* a prenup. "I'm not signing anything, Ryan. This is ridiculous. You're assuming this marriage won't last, and I'm offended you would even think that."

I sighed. "Alexis, really? You're really going to give me grief about this? After all the times we've broken up in the past, you're going to tell me you think that you and I are destined to be together forever?"

She gave me a look. "Oh, you have this attitude going in? What, are you going to say in your vows 'til divorce do us part?' Because that would be accurate for how you're feeling."

"No, I don't assume you and I will be divorced. But you have to observe some rules I'm going to lay down. Otherwise, yes, you and I will end up in divorce court. Sooner, as opposed to later."

She got quiet and just looked at me expectantly.

"Okay, first off – you have to stay off illegal drugs and on your meds. Second, and I can't believe I have to say this out loud, as it should just be a matter of common sense, but I need you to not sleep with other men. Third, you're going to stay on a budget. *We're* going to stay on a budget."

"What? I can hang with the other stipulations, but why, on God's green earth, are we going to have to budget? You have an endless supply of money, probably more than one person can spend in a lifetime."

"We're going to budget, and that's that. I'm not saying we have to be frugal, but I know you, Alexis, and I know that you can spend money like water. *My* money like water. You always have. You need to learn to manage money better." I didn't say the words, but the meaning was clear – there might come a time when Alexis didn't have my "endless supply of money" at her disposal, so she needed to learn, sooner as opposed to later, how to budget.

She pouted. "Okay, I guess I'll be shopping at the Good-will from now on for clothes and Aldi's for groceries. I'll be sure to clip all the coupons out of the circulars as well, and I guess I'll DVR that show about the extreme couponers. We need to be sure, from now on, that we have a BOGO coupon for when we eat out."

I rolled my eyes. "Don't be ridiculous, Alexis. You can still have your designer labels and gourmet foods, but you don't need one hundred purses and you really don't need 1,000 pairs of shoes. Perhaps your purses don't have to be Prada and your shoes don't necessarily have to be Chanel. That's all I'm saying."

"Well, that's bullshit. You know I have to match my shoes and purses to my outfits. And, since I have so many outfits, I have to have purses and shoes to match. And you seem to expect me to make do with last year's accessories and clothes. You might think a Target purse is the same quality as an Hermés, but I'm here to tell you that simply isn't true. You really do get what you pay for, which is why I choose to pay for quality."

I was about to lose my patience. "Listen, Alexis, you're simply going to have to limit yourself. I'm going to put my foot down on this, because you spend way too much money. I'll allow you a healthy clothing and accessory budget of $10,000 a month. That's it. No more. And we're going to have to go over a monthly budget for entertainment, food and the like. You're not going to spend my money like it's going out of style anymore."

It was her turn to lose her patience. "$10,000 a month? $10,000 a month? I can buy like one Hermés purse with that and a couple of pairs of shoes. And that will be it. What about my suits and cocktail dresses and everything else I need for my job? What about that, Ryan?"

Alexis had just gotten her job at a high powered – and high dollar – law firm, and I knew she had to dress well there. "$10,000 a month, Alexis. You're just going to have to make do with that."

She crossed her arms. "And what about the baby? Do you expect me to dress our child in rags?"

"No, of course not. But it's not necessary for the baby to have all the latest fashions. Shop at Gymboree and Baby Gap and be done. She doesn't have to have the best of the best, and, in fact, I don't want her to. I don't want to spoil her. Or him."

"Ryan. You obviously don't know what pressure is on me to keep up with everyone else in our social circle. I have to keep up with what they're doing, and that means this child will have to have the best of everything. I don't want to be ostracized because of you."

"What social circle? You don't have friends, you have acolytes and acquaintances. Why do you give a crap what any of those women think, I'll never know." And that was true. Alexis had a healthy social life, full of parties and outings, but there wasn't a person who gave two craps about her. Most of them had no idea that she had a mental illness, which meant that, when she was in the throes of mania, the $10,000 budget I gave her would be gone in a matter of hours.

"Oh? You think Lisa, Karen and Sophia are acquaintances? They're my best friends, and their children have the best of everything. And their husbands don't limit their spending to $10,000 a month."

"No, I don't think those women are your friends." I narrowed my eyes. I *knew* those women weren't her friends, because every one of them had made a play for me. Every.one.of.them.

I wasn't going to tell Alexis that, though. It would crush her. Not to mention, make her spin off into a jealous tangent that would bring everybody down.

"Listen, Ryan, it's different for you. You're a man. You don't have the same types of pressures as I do, especially when it is going to come to our child. None of your guy friends are going to know, or care, if our child's crib comes from Nieman Marcus, but my girlfriends will."

I sighed. I was going to have to bring out my ace in the hole. "Okay, Alexis, fine. Don't agree to my terms. The wedding is off."

She narrowed her eyes, trying to gauge if I was bluffing. She tapped her fingers on the table and studied me. I made my face as blank as I could. Was I bluffing? On the one hand, marrying this woman was the last thing, the very last thing, I wanted to do.

On the other, I had to do right by the unborn child.

"$15,000 a month," she said.

"No deal. You're lucky I'm limiting you to ten."

"$10,000 a month for me and $10,000 a month for the new baby."

"Alexis. There's no justification for spending that kind of money on a baby. There's no justification spending that kind of money on a child or adolescent or even a young adult. I'll put plenty of money away for college, and pay for a nanny, but that's it."

"So, what? What kind of a budget do you want for the new baby?"

"I'll buy quality furniture for the baby, so an initial outlay of $10,000 would probably be sufficient. But, ongoing, for clothes and shoes and toys and diapers and all of that, I really think $2,000 a month should more than suffice."

"What? You've got to be kidding me. Unless you want to dress our child in rags –"

"Don't be dramatic. $2,000 a month is more than enough. There's my offer. Take it or leave it."

"I'm leaving it," she said.

"Okay. Well, then, forget it. I'll go and visit Sheldon tomorrow and have him draw up a petition to establish paternity, and you'll just have to live off the minimum child support I'll be required to pay by law. And we'll have shared custody. If that's how you want to play it, that's how it's going to be."

"Ha, I'll probably get more money out of you in child support than you're offering me, so let's go for it."

"Alexis. Talk to a lawyer. My assets won't go into a child support calculation. Only my income will. And, while I'm making six figures, my income doesn't come close to my assets. You're going to be disappointed, I can guarantee you that."

I could almost see the wheels turning around in her brain. She knew I was right. I was worth millions and I had millions in the bank – I was very liquid and I also had some serious assets that were non-liquid. But my salary didn't come close to what I owned and the child support would be based upon that.

"I can't believe you. I didn't know you were such a goddamned cheapskate."

"Alexis, I'm not. I'm a very generous guy." I hesitated a long time before saying anything more, but I finally did. "But we have to live in reality here. Chances are very good this marriage won't last. You'll end up cheating on me, or there will be some other deal-breaker down the road, and that will be it. Child or no child. Don't get me wrong – I want this to work, but only because there is a child involved.

But you might, someday, have to live without me, so you need to learn how to manage your money, just in case that happens."

Those words hung in the air. Alexis looked like she was ready to kill me. She just sat there, stewing and glaring at me. She opened her mouth, and then shut it again.

I think she knew she was defeated.

"Okay," she said.

Got that out of the way. Now the fun begins.

"Alrighty. Now, let's go over this prenup."

Chapter Four

As I suspected, Alexis threw an absolute hissy fit when she saw the terms of the prenup. "This is bullshit. If we divorce, I get nothing at all. This is absolute bullshit."

"Alexis, these are the terms of the agreement. You can take it or leave it."

"I'm leaving it."

"Okay."

She was pacing around the room. She almost seemed as if she were off her meds and was in the throes of a manic episode. "You can't do this to me, Ryan. Why would you want to leave me with nothing?"

"Alexis, stop being so dramatic. I'm not leaving you with nothing. After all, I put in the stipulation that you will get a $10 million cash settlement when we get divorced, no matter when we get divorced. We could be married one day and you would still get that." I talked Sheldon into putting this stipulation in. I knew Alexis. I had to put something in there to appease her, otherwise she was going to go Defcon 1.

"$10 million? You're worth fifty times that."

"I am not," I said, although I knew I was worth close to fifty times that amount. It all depended upon the value of the Cézanne, the de Kooning and the Benton. "Anyhow, what I'm worth is not relevant here. I think you know as much as I do that what you would be entitled to in a divorce settlement would not include my separate property, and, as of now, what I have is my separate property. Be happy I'm giving you $10 million if things go south."

"Goddammit, Ryan, you're such a cheapskate. I hate you. I really hate you."

I had no doubt that she did hate me, right at that moment. I often found myself hating her, as well.

"Be that as it may, Alexis, you have to take it or leave it. I'm tired of these fucking games."

She bit her lip. "Well, Ryan, what if I told the people at your work about your past?"

"What, about my drug use? I was up front with them about it. I'm not insured by their insurance company because of it, but that's okay. I have my own insurance. There's not much you can say to me that would hurt me."

"I'm not talking about that," she said. "I'm talking about what happened to you when you were young."

Something about those words made my blood run cold. "What happened when I was young? I mean, my father was abusive, but how is that anyone's business?"

She stared at me, as if she couldn't quite believe what I was saying. "You don't remember, do you?"

Things were getting too uncomfortable, all of a sudden. "I don't remember what?"

"Nothing," she said. "Nothing."

"Alexis, out with it. Go ahead with what you were going

to say. You obviously think you have dirt on me, so go ahead and tell me what that is."

"No," she said. "Far be it for me to freak you out by making you remember things you probably shouldn't. Anyhow…"

I wanted to press her further, but something stopped me. There was something there, I knew there was, lurking underneath the surface. I didn't want to face up to it, so I decided not to make her tell me what that thing was.

"Okay, whatever," I said. "Now, are you signing, or aren't you?"

"I'm going to take the prenup to my lawyer."

"Goes without saying."

"So, no promises," she said.

I had a feeling she was going to sign it.

I also had a feeling she wasn't going to be happy.

Chapter Five

Nick and I were finally going to meet for drinks. We hadn't talked since I found out he and Alexis had recently slept together. I decided it was time to rectify that.

"Let's meet at the Phoenix," I said, referring to the jazz club downtown. "At 8."

"I'll be there."

I had to catch him up on everything that was happening. Granted, it was happening fast, so I would imagine he would be feeling like he had whiplash from all the changes that were occurring between Alexis and me.

But, mainly, I was ready to talk. I was angry with him because he and Alexis had recently hooked up. But I figured it was time to get over that, as Alexis and I were officially broken up at the time, even though she and I slept together that one fateful time. That was enough for me to impregnate her, unfortunately.

We were all dysfunctional, I knew that. But I needed him as a friend. And he was back with Rielle, after having split with her for a matter of weeks, during which time he hooked up with Alexis. I was happy about that, as they had three small children, and he seemed to be truly ready to settle down.

Perhaps that was what we needed – for all of us to settle down. Mature. Grow.

I got there just a little bit early, and found a seat.

Then, to my amazement, I saw *her* again.

She was dressed down just a little, and it seemed she wasn't at all like Alexis in her taste in clothing. She didn't seem to go for the designer labels, and her purse seemed to not be high dollar. She just looked normal.

Yet stunning, to me, at the same time.

I was mesmerized and more than a little befuddled. Twice in one week? What are the chances?

I fought within myself not to go over and talk to her. Introduce myself and ask her name. Find out more about her. I still had no idea why I was so drawn to her, but I was. And she was put into my path not once, but twice.

I shook my head. I had committed to Alexis, and I was going to see it through. I had to.

But, at the same time, I thought that perhaps buying her a drink wouldn't be too out of the question. Would it?

My mind and my heart were at war with one another. Unfortunately, or maybe it was fortunate, things were settled for me, because she evidently had a date. She stood up as a guy entered through the front door, and she held out her hand. The guy nodded at her, and the two of them sat down.

I watched them from afar. I thought that perhaps, just perhaps, the two were on a blind date. After all, they didn't seem to be all that friendly with one another. The body language told me they weren't close.

I sipped my scotch and still felt conflicted. Everything

seemed to be against my meeting this woman, yet, at the same time, I so wanted to meet her. Something inside of me was screaming that I needed to meet her. For some reason. I didn't know exactly what that reason was, but no matter. There was something compelling me to meet her.

While I watched her, another woman came over to my table. Dressed in a low-cut blouse that showed off her ample cleavage, the woman was slender and blonde and gorgeous. In a husky voice she said "I noticed you were alone. I was wondering if I could join you?"

I looked at the woman politely. "Sorry, but, no. I'm waiting for somebody." I felt annoyed. I wanted to concentrate my energies on the mystery woman, but this other woman seemed to want to monopolize my attention right then.

"Too bad. Guy or girl?"

"Guy. I'm waiting for my friend."

She nodded. "Well, I'm at the table over there," she said, pointing to a table that was full of women. "If you would like to come over and say hello."

"Okay," I said. Sometimes the female attention got annoying. I could never go anywhere, it seemed, without somebody trying to flirt with me.

I looked at my watch. Nick was running late, evidently, but not too late.

Over at the table where the mystery woman sat, the guy had gotten up and left. Probably just went to the bathroom or to get a drink, but perhaps it was time for me to get up and make my move. So, I went over and brushed past her table.

I stood about ten feet away and watched her, charmed by the way the swayed to the music and how much she really seemed to be into it. At the same time, she had a certain awkwardness about her. It was hard to place, but she seemed perpetually out of sorts. Like she was when I first saw her on the street. She didn't quite seem to be as together as Alexis tried to be, and I liked that.

I still had no idea why this woman had such a strong effect on me. I only knew she did.

Then Nick came through the door.

I took my seat and gestured to him. "Nick, over here," I said. He saw me, nodded, and headed on over.

"Hey," he said. "I'm really glad you called."

"Me too," I said. "I'm still not happy with you, but I thought you needed to know what's going on with Alexis and me."

"Okay," he said. "Let me guess. She's preggers and you guys are getting married." At that he smiled. It was obviously a joke.

"Well, I guess you beat me to the punch. Because that's exactly what is happening."

He looked at me like he thought I was shitting him. "Oh, right. Listen, this isn't a funny joke."

"Who's laughing?" I said. "I wish it were all a joke, but, no. She's pregnant, I'm the father and we're getting married."

He looked stunned. "What? This is not a joke?"

"Nope. Not a joke."

He shook his head. "Well, then, what the hell? So she's knocked up. Why would you be getting married to her? News flash, getting married isn't what's expected these days. In fact, in your case, getting married isn't even what's advisable. You need to think twice about this one, buddy. Seriously."

"I know what you're saying," I said to him. "I really do.

And I agree with you. But it's happening. So I thought it was time to mend fences with you."

"You want me to be your best man?"

"Nah. We aren't doing all that. We're going to get married in front of a judge. There's not a need for all that speaking of the vows crap, because you and I both know it would all be bullshit anyhow."

"Well, you're crazy. And the stupid thing is that you're the romantic guy who really has always believed in true love. That was what you always said to me, anyhow, when you were drugged up in college. Now you're telling me you're going to settle for a woman that you not only don't love, but don't even like. What's up with that?"

"Sometimes you have to do something that isn't in your best interest, but, rather, is for the greater good. You know?"

"How is getting married for the greater good here? You're going to bring a child into your dysfunction? God, Ryan, I would think that you would know better than that. I would think that you would know better than to repeat the mistake of your parents."

"Ironically enough, that's why I'm doing this. Because of my parents. Because I want this new baby to have the chance for happiness that I never did. So, you can support me or not, but I'm doing this."

He shook his head and went back to his drink. "I don't support you in this. I support you, though, in general. But I'm registering my objections to this unholy union right here and right now."

"Duly noted," I said. "And, I'll be honest with you. I know you're completely correct in objecting to this. I do believe in true love. And I do think my being with Alexis forecloses that. But I'm a responsible guy and I don't walk away from my mistakes."

My eyes wondered over to the mystery woman, who was now sitting by herself. It seemed as if the guy who joined her earlier had cut and run, because he had been gone from her table for quite awhile. She now looked sad and lonely and my heart went out to her. I wondered what happened – did she arrange to meet somebody there, and he snuck out when she wasn't looking?

She intrigued me more than Alexis ever did.

I suddenly realized Nick had said something to me, and I had no idea what he just said. "So, buddy, what do you think about that?"

"I'm so sorry, I just lost you. What were you saying?"

He looked at me suspiciously, and then looked over at the mystery woman.

"What the hell? You were completely zoned out a second ago and you were distracted by that girl down there. Who, by the way, is completely not your type."

I felt myself turning red. "I'm sorry, I was looking for our waitress. What were you saying?"

"I was simply saying you shouldn't abandon your new baby, but you should see a lawyer about establishing paternity, child support and visitation. That way, you're not saddled to her, and you can still be in that child's life."

"What a great idea. Why didn't I think of that?" I asked, sarcasm dripping from my voice. "Seriously, I did think about that, but I think that providing, at least trying to provide, a stable home for this baby is the best thing to do."

"Okay," he said. "Now, do you want to tell me why you've been so fixated with that redhead down there?"

Nothing escaped Nick, unfortunately. "I don't really know why," I said. "I've seen her now twice, and, well…"

He waited, expectantly, for me to finish my thought.

I took a deep breath. "Have you ever seen somebody,

just a random person, and you feel like you know that person. But you really don't? You've never seen the person in your entire life?"

He shrugged. "I guess." By the look on his face, I knew he never actually had that happen to him. "Why? You feel you know that woman, but you really don't?"

I shook my head. "Yes. I can't really even explain it. It's like these talk shows where people come on, psychics, and they talk about how sometimes you encounter people who you've known in your past lives."

Nick was now giving me a look like he wanted to commit me. "Okay. So, now you're talking about psychics and astrologers and all those other charlatans who only want your hard-earned money. Like that John Edwards dude, or whatever his name is."

"John Edward. John Edwards was the sleazy politician who cheated on his dying wife."

"Yeah, that guy. The guy who sees dead people," he said with a chuckle.

"I didn't think you would understand," I said. I then hesitated awhile and took a few sips of my drink. "There was something that happened to me, a few years back, that makes me believe there might be something out there. Something beyond our understanding or our comprehension."

Nick raised his eyebrows. "Do tell."

I took another deep breath. "Well, you know how I was locked in a car trunk for three days by those drug dealers?"

"I remember."

"I never really told you how I got out of there."

"No, you didn't. I guess I always just assumed that you got out of the trunk because they eventually let you out. They were only trying to scare you."

"Actually, that wasn't what happened. I heard a voice when I was in that trunk. It was a voice that belonged to an old woman. She knew my name, and told me it wasn't my time. She also told me that my daughter needed me. I didn't have any children, of course, that I knew about."

"Okay. You were obviously hallucinating. That isn't exactly a surprise, considering you were locked in a trunk for three days without food or water and you were coming off drugs. Plus, you were freaking out."

"That's just it. I would have thought the same, except those guys who were outside the car door, the ones who kept threatening to set the car on fire – they saw this woman, too. One of them called her a witch, and said they needed to get out of there. And they took off, and this woman was able to pop the trunk open. She didn't have a key or anything."

"You hallucinated them calling her a witch, too. Hell, you probably hallucinated the whole incident. You were pretty whacked-out in those days."

"No, I didn't hallucinate the whole incident. I talked to Seth about it, and he confirmed that I was forced into a car trunk. And these guys were serious. I don't think that they would have burned me up in that car, as that kind of punishment is reserved for serious rats, but they obviously had it in for me - I was a witness and I was hanging out with Seth, who was apparently poaching their boss' clients."

"And what happened to Seth?"

"He was tortured. But he lived, of course, and he was very careful from that point on not to encroach on that other dealer's clients."

He raised an eyebrow. "So you're saying this woman.."

"Saved me from something horrible, like what Seth ended up going through. Being in the car trunk was bad enough, but much worse might have happened if she didn't intervene."

"So, you got lucky. Some old crone appeared at just the right time and scared those two dudes away."

"No. These were some rough guys. They had machine guns. They weren't the kind to just be afraid of some random old woman. They sensed something about her, something other-worldly, and they didn't want to fuck with her."

Nick looked like he was growing impatient of this entire story. "Listen, Ryan, there's some logical explanation for that encounter. I'm sure of it."

"Yeah, but the weird thing was that she literally disappeared. Into thin air. I tried to thank her for saving me, and she disappeared." I shook my head. "There are some things in this world that simply cannot be explained by logic, and that encounter was one of those things."

"You sound like a nut."

"Think what you want, I don't really care."

"Okay. Let's just say for the sake of argument that the old woman who helped you was some kind of a spiritual guide or something of the sort. I'm not saying that I believe that at all, but you seem to. For whatever reason. Let's just say that she is. What does she have to do with that redheaded woman here at this bar?"

I shrugged. "I don't know. Maybe nothing. Maybe everything. I just feel like I know her. I have a strong feeling that I've met her before and that maybe…"

"Maybe what?"

"Nothing," I said. Nick would think that I was nutty if I told him that I thought that maybe this woman was some-how…somebody that I was supposed to be with.

I even sounded nutty to myself.

"Let's change the subject," I said to him. "I'm going to be a father. Isn't that great?"

"Yeah," he said, without enthusiasm. "It would be if the mother wasn't such a fucking lunatic. But, hey, I admire you for stepping up the plate. I just hope you know what you're doing."

"I do," I said. Then I put my hand on his shoulder. "I'm really happy we're talking again. I know it's bullshit what happened back at that house, but I think you know it too. At any rate, it's all water under the bridge, isn't it?"

"I hope so," he said. "Anyhow, I'm not in the market for Alexis anymore, or anybody else. I'm going to commit myself to Rielle."

"Right," I said. "Well, I wish you good luck with that."

"Maybe I need it," he said. "But, at some point in a man's life, he has to stop chasing tail and finally settle down. Rielle's pretty cool, I guess. We'll see how it goes."

We clinked glasses, two old buddies who once again were close friends.

And I tried, for the rest of the evening, to put that mystery woman out of my mind. It was difficult, but I had to do it.

I was going to be married, and that was that.

Chapter Six

Alexis and I got married in a quickie ceremony, and she moved in right away. Nobody that either of us knew even went to the courthouse to wish us well. Not that we expected that. Pretty much everyone was against it.

I held my breath, though, when I went to the courthouse. There was a part of me that was hoping to catch a glimpse of my mystery woman. After all, she was an attorney, and it appeared that her offices were around the courthouse area, so it wouldn't be too terribly coincidental for her to be around.

Nonetheless, if she had showed up anywhere near where Alexis and I got married, I probably would have called the whole thing off and gotten the mystery woman's phone number. I would have finally seen it as a definitive sign that this entire thing with Alexis was wrong-headed and would end in disaster.

But she didn't show. Mystery woman wasn't anywhere around that I could see. So, we went on ahead and got our marriage license, went in front of the judge, and got it done.

Alexis was quiet afterwards, though.

In the car, I asked her what was on her mind.

"Oh, well, this was supposed to be my special day. I had dreamed of it since I was a little girl. And the way we did it was so anticlimactic. So sterile. You didn't even kiss me."

I took her hand and kissed it. "I know. And I'm sorry. But I didn't want to pretend this is something it's not. We're not marrying because we're in love, and I think that you know that. There's no use making it an even bigger charade by having some huge ceremony and taking vows and all of that."

There were tears in her eyes. "You don't love me now. But maybe you will? Maybe we can grow to love one another?"

"Sure," I said. "You have to keep it together, though, like we talked about. No cheating, stay on your meds." Even as I said those words, though, they felt hollow. The sad story was that I really didn't like who Alexis was. It wasn't even her behavior that turned me off. It was her essence – her ethics, her morality, and what was important to her. None of these things matched up with me and who I was.

In order for me to truly love her, she was going to have to change who she was. And I knew that was not only impossible, but unfair for me to ask that of her.

So, in my mind, this was a marriage of convenience, and it always would be. But hopefully we could like one another, and get along well enough, that we could provide a good home for the baby.

SEVEN MONTHS LATER, MIA WAS BORN. And my world was instantly changed. I suddenly knew that my sacrifice in marrying Alexis was worth it. One hundred percent worth it. This was my child, and I wasn't a part-time father. I was completely in Mia's life, and I was completely, head over heels, in love with her.

Alexis and Mia came home from the hospital, and the room was already furnished and waiting for her. Alexis and I had compromised on the furniture – she got the armoire, the chest of drawers and the rocking chair that she wanted. I got the crib I wanted – I wanted something that I could put together, with my own hands. I wanted that memory. That was important to me, so Alexis and I got a beautiful solid cherry crib that was disassembled, and we spent most of the day assembling it. When it was all done, I felt proud of what we had accomplished. And the crib was beautiful.

As was Mia herself. She was blonde, blue-eyed and beautiful. I knew instantly that she belonged to me – I didn't need the DNA test results to tell me this. For one thing, she looked like a Gallagher – she was the spitting image of Sarah when Sarah was a little baby. But, more importantly, she felt connected to me. Like she was a part of me.

For Alexis' part, she was at least a tiny bit maternal. She wasn't what I had envisioned for the mother of my child, but she tried. And that was really enough.

She didn't breast feed, of course. "Oh, God, no," she said, when I brought up the topic to her. "I need these babies to go back to the way that they were as soon as possible," she said, holding her breasts in her hands for emphasis. "I don't want to go around with saggy tits."

I went over to her, and tried to put my hands on her breasts, but she rebuffed me. "You can't see me like this," she said to me. "I look hideous."

"You look beautiful," I said to her, and I meant it. She *was* beautiful. She was objectively beautiful, which means that everyone I knew found her beautiful. As opposed to subjectively beautiful, which is the kind of person who is beautiful to a select group of people, but not to others.

The redhead, who I was still a bit obsessed with, would fall into the latter category. There was something about her that I found absolutely stunning, although I knew that, to the rest of the world, she probably would be considered to be merely cute.

Alexis, on the other hand, was stunning to just about anybody.

Yet, here she was, in front of the mirror, obsessing about the way that she looked. "Ugh," she said, grabbing her belly, which had just a bit more heft to it than before she got pregnant. "I need to go Keto like yesterday." And then she grabbed her breasts. "And if these don't bounce back, I'm going to be seeing a plastic surgeon."

"Alexis," I said. "You're gorgeous. Why are you obsessing about all of this? You just had a baby. You're allowed to look a bit imperfect for awhile."

"Fuck that," she said, as she hoisted a celebrity magazine in front of my nose. "Look at this actress. She has had three children and she just popped out her latest. Not one ounce of fat on her." She shook her head. "If she can do it, I can do it."

I sighed. "You do know that PhotoShop can make these actresses look much better than they really do in life? And, even if this particular actress really does look amazing in real life, she gets this way through trainers and personal chefs and, if all else fails, starvation. You're a real woman. You're not a celebrity. You're a lawyer. And you're still a size 6. So lighten up already."

She started crying. "A size 6. I'm a fucking cow. Before I pushed out this crying brat, I was a size 2. A size 4 at the most." She shook her head. "I need to get to the gym and I need to eliminate all carbs for awhile. Sorry about that."

I sighed. Alexis was a bit maternal, but she was still very much into herself. Her maternal instincts went in the direction of picking up Mia when she cried and rocking her to sleep, and bottle feeding her whenever she was hungry.

The diapers were changed by me, however. That much was established early on. If I was home, I was on diaper duty.

And I was loving every minute of it.

When I was at work, Alexis had a nurse come in to help her. The nurse changed all of the diapers.

"Thank God for Dana," Alexis said to me, referring to the nurse. "I don't know what I would do without her."

I shook my head. Alexis had not yet gone back to work, so I had to admit that I couldn't quite understand why she needed the extra help. Women all over the world were able to take care of children on their own, why couldn't she?

But I didn't protest. Things were actually kind of peaceful between Alexis and me. I didn't really want to make waves, and I had the money to hire the full-time nurse, so there wasn't a problem there. And Alexis would be back at work soon enough, so it was probably best to have the nurse established and in the home, so that there would be a seamless transition when Alexis went back to work, and the nurse had to be there alone with Mia.

One thing was for sure – I was finally happy. I couldn't think of a time in my life when I was truly happy. I had been dealing with drug addiction for so long, and there were nightmares that plagued me throughout my life. Nightmares about things I didn't even really know about, but my subconscious mind did. And, even when I got off the drugs, the depression was always there. I was getting therapy, but nothing really seemed to help.

But Mia brought sunshine into my life. I never really thought that it would be possible to feel this deeply about another person. That I could feel this pure about another person. She brought out the very best in me.

She was growing up a little every day, and I could already tell that she was special. She was very small, but she seemed to be aware of things around her. Much more aware than I would expect an infant to be. She really seemed to understand what I was saying to her. It could have been my imagination, but she really did seem to know, listen and understand when people were speaking.

Because of Mia, my life would have been idyllic.

It would have been, but Alexis managed to screw that up. Like she always did.

Chapter Seven

Looking back on it, I couldn't really blame Alexis. She was trying, and she was finally considering breast-feeding baby Mia. "I can't stand the pressure," she said. "All the mommies I know are all judging me for not doing it. My breasts will bounce back, I guess."

I didn't think that was a sound reason for breast-feeding Mia, but, at the same time, I was happy that Alexis was coming around on this. I knew all the studies about how babies who are breast fed get fewer infections, developed fewer allergies, were protected against obesity, and also supposedly were more intelligent than bottle-fed babies.

"Alexis, I guess I don't understand. Mia is now four months old. I don't think you can start breast-feeding now. I think you had to start doing that when the baby was first born."

"I know that, Ryan. That's why I've been pumping my breast milk. I haven't shared that piece of information with you, but I've pumped every day so that the milk doesn't dry up. I haven't told you about this, because I didn't want you to pressure me about my decision. But I wanted to have the option of breastfeeding her if I changed my mind. And, well, I changed my mind. So, I'm ready to do this."

There was one major problem with this, of course.

"I'll have to go off my meds," she said. "Of course."

Why that didn't occur to me before, I don't know. I guess I wasn't really thinking about it that much.

But, suddenly, I was very concerned. "Alexis, maybe we should re-think this."

"Re-think what? Listen, I'm tired of getting the stink-eyed looks from these holier-than-thou women. I'm going to try to breast feed her, but I do need to get off the meds for at least a few weeks before I attempt that."

I knew what would happen if she went off her meds. And I knew that she would be at increased risk for all kinds of mental issues, considering her history of profound bi-polar behavior, combined with the fact that her hormones were out of whack. "Alexis, please listen to me. You can't go off your meds."

"Oh, I'll be fine. I've been fine for what, years now? I haven't had any incidents where I've had to be hospitalized in a long time. I don't think I need the meds anymore."

"You do need the meds. You're just experiencing what many people with mood disorders experience – you think you're cured when you can never really be cured. You'll always have to be diligent with your meds, just like a diabetic needs to take insulin. And you're dangerous without them."

"Well, I'd rather be dangerous than be shunned by my social circle. Those women can be catty if you don't do things the way they think they should be done."

We argued about this issue, round and round, as I tried to convince her not to go off her meds, and she tried to convince me that she would be fine without them.

"Listen, Alexis, the baby might be fine if you continue to take them. After all, you took them while you were pregnant."

"Well, I wasn't feeding her the meds while I was pregnant. I will be if I take the meds now."

"Let's talk to your doctor about this," I said.

She rolled her eyes. "I already did, at the last well-baby checkup. He told me the meds that I'm taking didn't pose a huge risk to Mia when she was a fetus, but will pose a risk to Mia if she's exposed to them through my milk. I don't want to take that chance."

I paced the floor and Mia started crying. "I need to go and get her," I said, as Alexis made no move towards her room.

"No," she said. "Let her cry it out."

"Why would I let her cry it out? She probably needs something. We need to at least check and see why she's crying before we just dismiss her."

"We need to finish our discussion," Alexis said to me.

"We are finished. I told you when we got married that you need to stay on your meds and I meant that. I'm sorry that you're being shunned by your girlfriends, but your mental health is more important and should take precedence over the risk of a social stigma."

"So what are you saying? If I breastfeed our child, which, I might remind you, is going to give her a huge boost later on in life, you're going to leave me? What kind of a person are you?"

"I'm somebody who doesn't want to deal with you when

you're not taking your meds. I've been there way too many times before, Alexis, and it usually ends up with you over-dosing on your illegal drug of choice or in jail. And then on to the mental institution. I'm very sorry that you're dealing with this illness, and I know it's not fair, but you are. You are, and you have to be diligent with it."

She opened her mouth to argue, and I shut her down. "It's non-negotiable," I said to her. "You either stay on your meds, or I will divorce you."

And, at that, I left Alexis and went to attend to our crying daughter.

MY ULTIMATUM DIDN'T GO OVER WELL with Alexis, at all. In fact, she stopped speaking to me over it. After we had our conversation about how she needed to stay on her meds, and not breastfeed Mia, she started to lock herself in the guest room for hours on end.

The upshot of that was that Dana, the nurse, was hired to tend to Mia full-time. I was working long hours, but I tried to take care of Mia when I was home. Alexis wasn't even trying anymore. She had completely lost interest in Mia, it seemed.

And she had completely lost interest in me, as well.

I suspected she was off her meds, anyway, or, even worse, she was back doing illegal stuff. I didn't really know. She was impossible to reach. I would go into her locked room with my spare key, and she would be lying in the bed, staring at the wall.

"Alexis," I said to her. "You need to come out of this room. There is a baby who isn't going to know you. That's your baby, I might add. She's going to think Dana is her mother."

She cocked her head. "So, what's the big deal? You had a nanny raising you after your mother left."

That was true, but that wasn't the ideal situation at all. "I know I did, but I never forgot my mother and never stopped wondering what happened to her. And I never stopped loving her. I felt, for so many years, that she just rejected me. I think that's the reason why I'm so screwed up these days."

She narrowed her eyes. "That's one of the reasons why you're screwed up for sure. But I can't believe you don't even remember the real reason why you're screwed up."

I shook my head. "I don't know what you're talking about."

"Well, maybe you need to concentrate on your own shit before you try to interfere with mine."

"What shit are you talking about? My mother is a schizophrenic and she's in the mental hospital. She left when I was very small. That would screw up anyone."

Alexis shook her head. "Goddamn it, Ryan, do you really think that's the sole reason why your head is messed up?"

"Well, no. I mean, my father was physically abusive to me, as well. But I think my mother is the main reason why I turned to the drugs."

"Think what you want," she said. "I know differently."

I took a deep breath. There was a nagging inner voice that told me that Alexis spoke the truth. That there was something worse, much worse, than my mother's rejection and my father's beating me.

And I had no desire to go there.

"Well, I have no idea what you're talking about, and, anyhow, we aren't talking about me, are we?"

"No, we're not," she said. "I mean, I would love to talk

about you for once, instead of always trying to focus on myself and my own failings. But I can't possibly be the one who is going to spin you down that rabbit hole. So, okay. Go off on me. I know you want to."

"I don't want to. I simply am trying to say that…"

"That what? That I'm an awful mother? That I can't do anything right?" Then she started to cry. "Goddamn it, I wish I could feel something for that little baby. I really do. I know I told you that I only wanted to breastfeed her because I'm getting pressure from my girlfriends about it, but that's really secondary. I really want to breastfeed her because I want to feel something for her, and I hoped that would be the best way to do that. But you've taken that away from me and now I have nothing left."

"Alexis, I don't know what to say to you. I think you have a classic case of postpartum depression, and, really, that's to be expected." I paused. "I made an appointment for you to see a doctor, Alexis. You need to see somebody. If you won't see your psychiatrist about adjusting your meds, then you need to see a specialist. Somebody who specializes in postpartum depression. I found somebody who does this. I made an appointment for you, Alexis."

Alexis said nothing.

The room was dim, but not completely dark, so I went over to put the overhead light on. "Ryan, don't," she said to me. "Don't turn on that light."

I said nothing, but just went over and turned on the overhead light. She got up to try to forcibly keep me away from the switch, and, when I turned and looked at her eyes, I suddenly knew why.

In fact, everything had become clear in that moment. Her behavior over the past few weeks suddenly made sense to me.

"You're using," I said. "Goddamn it, Alexis, you're fucking using again."

"I don't know what you're talking about."

"Oh, good lord, like I wouldn't know when you're using. Goddamn it, Alexis. I feel like such a fucking fool. I've been trying to give you your space. I was going to make an appointment with your doctor to see if you could take something for postpartum depression. And it turns out that all you need is to get back into fucking rehab."

That's when things turned ugly.

"Oh, well, look who's holier than thou," she said to me. "After all the problems you've had with drugs, you're going to get after me about a little joint here and there?"

"A little joint?" I said. "Let me see your arms."

She folded her arms in front of your chest. "No," she said. "You can't see them."

"Let me see them," I repeated. "Alexis, now. You show me those arms right this very second, or I'll leave and never come back."

"Bullshit. You wouldn't abandon your child like that."

I knew she was right. I was very, very attached to that little girl, and just the thought of leaving her there, in the care of Alexis, who was clearly in the throes of another drug relapse, was unthinkable.

"I wouldn't abandon her. I would take her with me."

"You wouldn't dare," she said. "And you just try to find an attorney who will take a child from her mother. There's not a judge alive who would give you custody of the baby after all the problems you've had over the years."

"Oh? And if you had custody of the child, I would make you take random drug tests. So, I would imagine that, if push came to shove, you would end up letting me have custody of her."

51

She narrowed her eyes. "The judge would have to have a reason to order drug testing, you know. And you have no proof of anything. So go right ahead."

"Let me see those arms."

"No."

That was when I forcibly took her arms and held them, while she howled, screamed and bit me. She knew there was no use resisting me, just because I was so much bigger and stronger than her, but, in her rage, she really had the strength of somebody much larger than herself.

I ended up wrestling her down to the floor and pinning her. She slapped me and pulled my hair, and I pulled her hair right back.

I was going to see those arms if was the last thing I did.

I finally managed to get her sleeves up and I saw the track marks on her skin. "Okay, Alexis, that's it. You're going to rehab."

"Oh, no," she said, as I let her up. She ran into the other room and dialed 911.

"Oh, Christ," I said. "What the fuck are you doing?"

"I'm calling the police. You're abusing me."

I shook my head, but, sure enough, in a matter of minutes, I heard a police car screaming down our street.

A uniformed officer got out of the car and Alexis ran to him. She pointed to me. "He hit me," she said, turning on the tears. "And he forcibly got me down on the ground and pulled my hair."

The officer came up to me. "Hello, I'm Officer Alex Cates," he said to me. "That young lady just said you beat her. Is that true?"

"No, that's not true," I said to him. "I would never lay a hand on her."

I looked at Alexis, who was now talking to Officer Alex's

partner, who was a petite woman with dark blonde hair. *Oh, great, just what I need. A sympathetic woman. Sympathetic to Alexis, not to me.*

The officer said to me "let's go inside and talk, shall we?"

I invited him inside and I told him what happened.

"Okay," he said. "You wrestled her to the ground. And you admit you pulled her hair."

I nodded. I wanted to tell him that it took all my power and might to not actually haul off and hit Alexis. If ever there was a woman who deserved it, it was her. But I knew that I could never, ever do something like that to her or any woman. "I did pull her hair," I said. "But I didn't hit her."

"I'm sorry, but you're going to have to come with me," he said. "Not that I don't believe you, but it sounds like the two of you need, at the very least, a time-out."

"Fine," I said. I probably would end up in jail. Not that this was anything new. I'd been jail before. Once down in Mexico because I was caught trying to bring pot over the border, and once during my college days. That time, I had gotten into a bar fight while I was high, and both of us ended up in the tank for 24 hours.

I followed the officer to his car and we ended up driving down to the station. There, I was arrested – fingerprinted, mug shots, signed a statement, the whole nine. And I was put into a cell where I waited to be finished processing.

SOME NINE HOURS LATER, I was finally allowed to make a phone call. The person that I called, naturally, was Nick.

"Buddy, I'm in jail."

"Oh? What happened now?"

"I don't want to talk about it. But can you come and get me out?"

"I'm there. Give me at least a half hour. What's the bond?"

"$5,000."

"$5,000? You must have done something bad, huh?"

I tried not to lose it over the phone. I wasn't angry with Nick, of course, but my stupid wife. And I knew Nick was going to say "told you so." As well he should. "I did nothing. But…listen, I don't want to go into it. I'll tell you everything when you pick me up."

"I'll be there."

And he was. He showed up in less than a half hour and posted my bond. Soon after, the guard let me out of my cell, and I went into the waiting room, where Nick waited for me.

"Thanks buddy," I said to him. "I owe you."

"Don't worry about it. But do you mind telling me what happened?"

"I will in the car. Let's go."

We made our way to Nick's Mercedes, and got in.

"Okay," he said, as he started the car. "Out with it. What happened?"

I sighed. "Alexis. She's using again."

He nodded. "I figured that. I mean, I have no reason why I figured that was going on, but I know Alexis. She definitely has problems staying sober. It was only a matter of time before she got off the wagon."

"I know. But we have a child now. I guess I was naïve. I thought that maybe with us having a kid and being married that perhaps she would finally settle down." I shook my head. "Having Mia has only made things worse, really,

54

because now there's a baby who is going to suffer. An innocent child is going to suffer."

"You knew this was coming. Anyhow, how did you get into jail?"

"I asked to see her arms. She refused, so I wrestled her to the ground to try to see them. She pulled my hair and I pulled hers."

Nick looked like he was waiting for me to say more.

"Okay, go on. What else happened?"

"Nothing. She told the police, though, that I hit her."

"Well, you know what she's doing there, don't you?"

"I know. I know her. I think she's trying to keep me in the house, because she knows that, if I move out and try to get custody of Mia, no judge will give me custody if I have an assault charge on my record."

Nick put his finger on his nose. "Well, I guess I don't need to fill in the blanks after all."

I shook my head and looked out the window. "Man, this sucks. I told her, before this assault bullshit happened, that I would leave her if she doesn't straighten up. We already had an issue with her wanting to go off her meds because she wants to breastfeed Mia. We had a fight about that a few weeks ago, and that was when she started to isolate herself from me. Locking herself in her room and that sort of stuff. Again, I feel naïve, but I really didn't imagine that she would be using again. But she is, and that's probably why she's been locking herself in her room all the time."

"So what are you going to do now?"

"Well, I'm going to call Sheldon, of course. I'm being arraigned for this tomorrow. In fact, I'm going to call him right now."

I did call him, and he agreed to meet me at the courthouse the next day.

I hung up. Nick was looking at me expectedly. "That's good that you have your lawyer coming to meet you tomorrow, but I need to know what you're going to do about Alexis and you and Mia. I think that you can see that you guys continue to be as toxic to one another as you always have been. You need to ditch that woman by the side of the road or you will not only never be happy, but you might start using again yourself."

I opened my mouth to say something but closed it again. I really had nothing to say. As usual, Nick was absolutely spot-on. "I'll have to see what happens with this assault thing. I have no doubt that I can beat it, but the problem is always that these things are he-said she-said, and Alexis can be pretty persuasive. Especially if the judge is a guy. So far, I've only been charged with a misdemeanor, but it's more than a little disturbing that I apparently have to answer the charge in the circuit court, not the city court, which means this charge is fairly serious. Serious enough that I might have an issue getting custody of Mia. And I can tell you one thing – if I can't get custody of her, then I need to stay right where I'm at. Because I cannot leave her alone with Alexis. That would be dangerous."

Nick looked at me and shook his head. "You're in it, aren't you? You really can't do anything. The saddest thing is that you're stuck in an unhappy marriage, when you could be with somebody who would actually make you happy."

I thought about the redhead and felt like crap. Why that woman was in my head, and had been ever since the day I saw her, I didn't know. But she was. And, every time I thought about how I was trapped in an impossible situation with Alexis, I thought of her.

"I know what you're saying. But I'm a responsible dad.

As long as Mia needs me, I'll do what's best for her. And, right now, what's best for her is having me in her life on a full-time basis. Unfortunately, right now, Mia and Alexis are a package deal."

"Well, then, you need a plan that assumes that you and Alexis will be staying together. What will that be?"

"I need to try to get her back into rehab for the zillionth time, and talk to her doctor about changing her meds. It can't be helping her mental health that her hormones are out of whack right now. I'll figure it out. I have to."

Nick was uncharacteristically quiet.

"What's on your mind?" I asked him.

"Well, you're the very definition of insanity. A walking, talking definition of insanity. Because you continually do the same thing over and over and expect a different result. Alexis will never change. You have to accept her craziness or get out."

"I changed."

"You were ready to change. That's the difference. She obviously isn't ready to change. And, until she gets ready to change, you're going to be pounding your head into a brick wall. I know this. I learned this with you."

I nodded my head. "I know."

"Yes, you do know. You know how hard I tried, all those years, to get you off drugs. Interventions, chaining you to your bed to forcibly detox you, getting you into rehab – none of that did any good. It wasn't until you were good and ready to get off drugs that you finally did get off them. It's the same with Alexis. I'm sorry to have to talk to you like this, but you need to hear it. She won't change. Accept her or fight like hell to get Mia, so that you can get out and finally be happy for real."

I sighed. I had no idea how I was going to get out of this

marriage. I supposed that if I beat the assault charge that I might have a bit of a chance to get full custody of Mia. But Alexis was right – I had quite a checkered past with my drug use and all that went with it. She was the mother, which would make it all the more difficult for me to get custody of my daughter.

I only hoped Sheldon could get me out of the assault charge. If he could, I might have a chance.

Chapter Eight

I showed up for court the next day, meeting Sheldon at the courthouse. I was embarrassed to be there, to say the very least, and more than a little bit pissed off. I had some time to think about what was happening, and I felt angry that I was put into this position by the world's most manipulative woman.

And, of course, wouldn't you know? The mystery woman was there in court. She was sitting in the front row with a stack of files on her lap. Her hair was loosely piled on her head and she was looking around the room.

My heart quickened as I thought that maybe we would make eye contact. But, at the same time, my being in court for an assault charge wouldn't exactly endear her to me. I felt like a criminal.

She stood up and greeted a guy coming in the door. "Hello, my name is Iris Snowe, and I'll be your public defender," she said, extending her hand to the young black male who was dressed in slacks, a dress shirt and slightly scuffed loafers.

"Jamal Brown," he said.

And then the two of them sat down, and she was evidently going over the procedure on what was about to happen with young Jamal. I heard snippets of conversation, as she handed him a file and went over the charges with him and what was going to happen.

At some point, she got up and went in a door. Another attorney greeted her and she said "I'll talk to you in a bit. Right now, I have to go into the tank."

"Good luck in there," the other attorney said.

"Yeah. I hate doing that, but I have some clients back there too."

I felt slightly amused watching her. She seemed to be frazzled and disorganized, but, at the same time, when I listened to her talking to Jamal, I knew she was smart and competent.

She came back out of the door, and started talking to the other attorney. I heard her whisper "oh my God. I don't believe this. That guy in handcuffs who was just brought in was a law school classmate." She pointed to a guy who was brought in, handcuffed to about five other guys, and was sitting in the jury box. "Crap," she said, "I don't want him to see me. He'll be so humiliated."

"It's okay, Iris," the other guy said. "Just go back into the tank if you want. I don't think your clients will be called until after the people with private attorneys go."

She nodded and went back into the door.

I held my breath, hoping she would reappear, but she didn't.

I had mixed emotions about this. On the one hand, I really wanted to see her again.

On the other, I was humiliated even being in that court.

The judge came in and everybody rose to their feet. The

bailiff announced "Division 33 is now in session, Judge O'Neill presiding. God save the State of Missouri and this honorable court."

I knew the drill. The judge would read me my charges and would give me a new court date to appear. I knew this, because Sheldon had informed me this was going to happen.

I drew a breath as the judge called my name. I looked nervously towards the bench where the red head, whose name was apparently Iris, was sitting. I hoped she wouldn't come back out, because nothing was more embarrassing than standing in front of a judge, being read charges.

I approached the bench with Sheldon. "Mr. Gallagher," the judge intoned, "you have been charged by the State of Missouri with assault in the second degree. How do you plead?"

"Not guilty, your honor," I said.

He nodded. "Your case, then, will be set for a preliminary hearing on April 11, at 9 AM, in this court. Good day, Mr. Gallagher," he said.

And, just like that, it was time to go.

WE GOT OUTSIDE OF THE COURTHOUSE, and I turned to Sheldon. "Okay, so the preliminary hearing is where the judge decides if there's enough evidence to advance the case to trial, right?"

"Yes," he said. "I'll call you to the stand and Alexis. I'll cross examine her forcefully, but you have to know that most of these cases advance to trial, no matter how well the preliminary hearing goes." He paused. "And you know these cases are tough. If Alexis is a good actor, she might be hard to shake."

"I don't think she wants me to go to jail. If you ask me, I think she's doing this as an insurance policy – she wants to have something on me in case there's a custody battle upcoming. Which there might be. I hope there isn't, but if she can't get off drugs, then I'll have no choice."

"That sounds about right," Sheldon said.

He should know. He knew Alexis well. Sheldon had been my attorney for a long time, so he knew both of us and how bad how relationship was.

"But, even so, even if Alexis' end game in this situation is to force me to stay, that doesn't matter. It doesn't matter, because she's going to fight like hell to make sure this charge sticks to me. What kind of a chance do I have to just walk away from this?"

"Well, you gave a statement to the police where you admitted that you wrestled her to the ground and you pulled her hair. That statement shows you technically assaulted her. But I should be able to get the charge reduced down to an infraction as opposed to a misdemeanor. That would mean a suspended sentence, and I probably can get it to where the charges are dismissed if there are no other incidents in a year. That would certainly help, because this whole thing won't go on your permanent record."

I shook my head. "And, what, during that year, I'll have a record? Sheldon, I don't think that will work. I'm already thinking about getting out of my marriage with Alexis, and I need to know I can get custody of Mia. How can I get custody of Mia if I have a record of assaulting her mother?"

"I would think you have more dirt on Alexis than she does on you."

"What kind of dirt? Yes, she's been to rehab, but so have I. The only thing is that she's been in and out of the mental hospital for her bi-polar disorder, but I would imagine that information would be tough to get because of privacy laws."

"Tough to get, but not impossible. When was the last time she was hospitalized?"

"Five years ago." I looked at Sheldon's face, and knew that that particular hospital stay was probably too long ago to make a difference in the custody case. "Yeah, that was awhile ago. She's going to make a good case that she's recovered and on her meds now."

"We can order that she take random drug tests."

I shook my head. "She knows how to beat those tests. She's been doing it for years. She's beaten every random drug test that her employers over the years have given her, even though she was a daily user. I'm quite sure she will beat them in the future, too."

"Well, it looks like this is going to be a crap shoot. Talk to her. See if you can work something out. As you probably know, if this was a more serious incident – like if Alexis were truly injured – the prosecutor's office wouldn't drop the charges on her say-so. But, in this case, since the charges are relatively minor, I would imagine that the case will go away if Alexis wants it to. Food for thought."

Food for thought. I was going to have to control my temper and talk to my wife. Talk to her about dropping the charges. Maybe come to some kind of agreement.

One thing was for sure, she had neutralized my leverage. I thought that I had the upper hand, because I could always walk out of the marriage, with Mia in tow, if push came to shove. Now, I didn't exactly have that ace in the hole.

"Well, Sheldon, I know you have to get back to work. And I really should as well. So, I'll be in touch. At any rate, assuming these charges aren't dropped, I'll be seeing you on April 11 for the preliminary hearing."

Sheldon nodded. "Good to see you, Ryan, as always. Too bad it couldn't be under better circumstances."

"Yeah, too bad."

At that, the two of us went our separate ways.

Chapter Nine

IRIS

I got home after another grueling day of seeing criminal clients, happy that I was soon going to be off that merry-go-round. Well, I guess I shouldn't say "merry go round," because it really was anything but merry. The pay sucked, too, and I wasn't doing well on my job. Truth be told, being an attorney was shaping up to be, more and more, a job that I simply wasn't cut out for.

That was because my brain wasn't wired for it. There were too many technicalities and intricacies in my job. Too many land-mines that were going to trip me up, sooner or later. I didn't mind going to the jail and seeing the men and women. I didn't mind the constant desperate phone calls and the pleas that they didn't do it, some other dude did it. I actually kind of liked that aspect of the job.

It was the other stuff that I couldn't hang with. The staying on top of dockets and writing constant motions for whatever comes up. I actually wouldn't have minded the motions if I could have used some kind of creativity and ingenuity in them. But these were pretty rote motions – no creative argument was necessary or even wanted.

I would have done better in the appellate division of the public defender's office. That would have been more my speed, because I always loved to research and I always loved to come up with arguments. I loved to write.

But, I knew that, since I wasn't doing well in the trial division, I certainly wouldn't be moved up to the appellate division. So, I knew that my days were numbered in this office.

I hoped I could do better on my own. Although, I had to admit that I was nervous about that. I had very little money in the bank, and I was going to have to hustle for every dollar. But it had to be better than the job I was at. It just wasn't a good fit.

I looked out the window to the parking lot below, and sipped on my jumbo-sized soft drink I got at the deli just below the building. And I became lost in thought.

I was drifting. That was the problem. There had been nothing in my life that made me feel as if I were on solid ground. Nothing in my life that made me feel in the least bit secure. I couldn't admit to myself that law school, in general, was probably a huge mistake. I put myself into enormous debt to get the law degree, and for what? So that I could make myself unhappy, a square peg trying to fit into a round hole, that's what.

And my love life. Oy, talk about depressing. I hadn't dated in a long time. Really dated, anyhow. I guessed I had gone on dates, usually with guys I met off of one of the Internet dating sites. And, so far, that was almost as disastrous as my professional life. I tried, I really did, to meet a good guy. But the term "good guy" seemed to be a contradiction in terms, thus far. There was always something amiss. Either there wasn't chemistry, or the guy was a jerk, or both.

I had to keep on trying. I wasn't getting traction anywhere, but what was my choice? If I gave up, then my life would go ahead and spiral into total disaster.

But if I kept swimming, then maybe, just maybe, I could get to shore. Perhaps there was something out there for me. A better job, or at least one that I liked. A good guy. I didn't necessarily think I would get the white picket fence or even a wedding ring. Just a good guy that I could hang out with, that maybe would turn into more. That was really all I asked for.

So, I was ever-hopeful. I had been corresponding with a guy over the Internet. He and I had written flirtatious e-mails back and forth for about a week. He seemed to be funny and intelligent and liberal, which was a definite bonus. He also was a good-looking guy and had a good job.

I tentatively asked if he wanted to meet, and he and I had made a date to meet up at a charity picnic on Saturday. The theme was "Lobsters and Lowenbrau," which really wasn't what was the menu. There weren't actually lobsters there, but there was Lowenbrau beer in a keg. It was an annual affair that was a benefit for a battered woman's shelter and it was usually well-attended. We arranged to meet there, because he had indicated that he was going to this function anyhow, and I was too. That way there really wasn't any pressure.

This was actually the first time I had been truly excited about meeting a guy in a long, long time. I couldn't remember when I had actually been jazzed about meeting somebody.

So, THAT FRIDAY, I BEGGED OFF WORK EARLY. I wanted to go shopping. I hadn't bought new clothes in quite awhile, and I wanted to buy something that looked okay on me, and also not like I was really trying. I had also saved up some money so that I could get my hair highlighted and low-lighted. I had done that before, and the results were really pretty – I had some strawberry-blonde chunks which were mixed deftly in with more coppery ones.

I spent the rest of that day patiently getting my hair done and shopping for something that was just right for a first meeting with somebody who had potential. I knew that I shouldn't get my hopes up. This date was probably going to turn out just like all the other ones, where I usually got a perfunctory email afterwards. If that.

I knew, going in, that it was going to be tricky. That one can never assume there is going to be chemistry in person, just because there seemed to be chemistry over the email airwaves.

Nevertheless, I liked this guy. I liked what he had to say in his emails. I liked his politics and his sense of humor. I liked his intelligence. Surely he wouldn't be like all the rest. Would he?

So, THAT SATURDAY, I pulled on my new clothes, checked my new hairdo in the mirror one more time, and headed out to the park. I was going by myself, but I would know people there. Nonetheless, it was going to be uncomfortable for me – I usually assumed that people didn't want to really talk to me, because I always found that I didn't really have much intelligent to say to people. I didn't know why I froze up in social situations. But I did. I always did. Especially if I was at a social situation I attended all by myself.

But I wanted to attend by myself. I felt I needed to. After all, if I brought a friend along, I might have to ditch her if I hit it off with Michael, which was the name of the guy I was meeting.

I made the calculated risk, therefore, to go to this place alone. So I did, and I got a beer and tried to make some small talk with some of the acquaintances that were there surrounding the picnic tables. But they pretty much shut me out, because I didn't know these people that well, and, as usual, I didn't have anything smart to say.

I slinked over to a picnic table that was unattended, sat on the table, and drank my beer alone. And I talked to myself. *He'll be here, Iris, he'll be here. And you guys will hit it off. This will be fun. You eventually won't be sitting here alone.* I checked my watch, and saw it read 1 PM. Michael was supposed to meet me there right at 1.

I drew a breath, remembering all the times I'd been stood up for a date. But I shook my head. That wasn't going to happen here. He confirmed this meeting with me. He seemed at least somewhat happy to meet me here. He was going to show.

At about 15 minutes after the hour, I saw him pull up in a white BMW. I recognized him from his picture as he emerged from the car.

And then I saw a thin blonde girl get out of the passenger's seat. And my heart sunk to my shoes.

I reluctantly got off the bench and stood up. He came over to me. "Iris?" he asked. He recognized me because I told him what I would be wearing and gave him a physical description of me.

"Yes, hello," I said. "Michael." I then looked over at the blonde girl. "I'm Iris," I said, holding out my hand, a smile plastered on my face.

"Kiera," she said. "I'm Michael's ex-girlfriend."

I was confused. He obviously had brought a buffer there to the picnic, but why would he bring his ex-girlfriend?

"Well, Iris," Michael said. "I'm going to get a beer. I'll catch you around, huh?"

I nodded and said nothing. And then started to talk to myself again. *Relax, Iris. At least he showed. He'll come over and talk to you after he gets his beer and he mingles. It's going to be okay.*

I drank the rest of my beer and went to the keg for more. Michael was talking to one of the hosts of the party and I went and stood right in front of him so he would know I was there and wanted to talk to him some more.

But he kept on talking to the guy he was talking to and didn't acknowledge me standing there. So I finished getting my beer and headed over to the picnic table again. And I looked around for somebody else who might want to talk to me. I saw lots of people I knew, but none who I would call a friend. And none who seemed to want to keep me company.

So I headed home.

Chapter Ten

RYAN

I didn't head right home. I also didn't go into work. I had to get my thoughts together before I went home and confronted Alexis.

How did I get into this mess? I loved Mia. I loved her more than I ever thought that I could love anybody. But there was a big part of me that regretted ever getting into bed with Alexis that one time.

Why did she and I end up in bed? After all, she and Nick slept together. She and I had never gotten along, ever. There wasn't any reason why I would have gone to her.

But I did. I did, and I regretted that. It was just something that was stupid. One of the stupidest things I'd ever done. Alexis wasn't whom I was supposed to be with. I knew that. It was becoming more clear to me every day that this was the case.

I felt nauseated.

I sat there drinking alone for the rest of the day. I shut off my phone and just drank one scotch after another. I made sure I found a dark table so that nobody would bother me. I didn't want to talk to anybody. I didn't want to see anybody. I just wanted to be alone with my thoughts and my alcohol.

I called Paul, my driver, to come get me at midnight. I was inebriated, and I was finally ready go home. I knew Alexis probably wasn't awake, but that was okay. I would just go on home and, in the morning, she and I would talk. I would just have to play a high-stakes game of chicken with her. It wouldn't be the first time I'd done that, and it wouldn't be the last, either. I was just going to have to convince her that I was serious about leaving if she didn't get help. Hopefully that would wake her up and make her see she needed help, and she would get it.

Again.

"Paul," I said when he answered the phone.

"Ryan," Paul said. He sounded strange. He and I were friendly, so I made sure he didn't address me as Mr. Gallagher. That name always made me feel old and pretentious. "Alexis has been trying to call you."

"I'm sure she has been. Anyhow, could you please come and pick me up? I'm at O'Malley's." This was a hole in the wall, and the place where I wanted to go whenever I wanted to be alone. I knew nobody would ever recognize me in there, which is why I always chose this particular place.

"Ryan," Paul said again. "I think you need to talk to your wife."

"I don't need to talk to her. Not right now."

But, to my shock, Alexis got on the phone. "Ryan," she said, her voice filled with tears. "I've been trying to get in touch with you for hours."

"For hours? I'm so sorry, Alexis, I've been at a bar contemplating things. I think we really need to talk. We need to figure things out, Alexis."

"Ryan, please come home."

"I am. That's why I just called Paul to come and pick me up. He's coming, isn't he?"

"Yes, Paul is coming," she said. "And you really need to come home right now."

"I am," I said. "Why do I have to repeat myself?" I was becoming annoyed with her and her questions. "I told you I'm coming home and I am."

"Good," she said. "I'll see you soon."

And she hung up.

I sat back down and waited for Paul to come and get me. He certainly seemed odd on the phone, as did Alexis, but I thought nothing of it. Alexis always sounded odd on the phone. At least she did most of the time. It certainly wasn't that peculiar that she sounded as if she had been crying. Because her crying was something I was more than used to. Alexis often spiraled into depression, and, when she did, she cried all the time.

PAUL came to get me and he and I made our way into the car. "Ryan, I'm taking you straight home," he said. "You need to talk to Alexis."

"I was talking to Alexis," I said. "Just now. Didn't you hear me talking to her?"

He nodded and said nothing more.

I got home and I entered the front door. Alexis was sitting on the couch, staring off into space. She had been crying, and I noticed that there were boxes of Kleenexes next to her on the coffee table. Tissues were wadded up and thrown around the living room.

I walked through the door, and she came up to me and

gave me a huge hug. "Oh, Ryan, Ryan, Ryan, I'm so happy you're here. I'm so happy."

"Okay, Alexis, of course I'm here. I said I would be. Now why the tears?"

"I don't know how to tell you this," she said. "I don't know how to tell you this."

"Tell me what?"

She looked at me, and then looked at her Kleenex again. She started to cry hysterically once more.

"What is it, Alexis?" I asked her. I wasn't all that disturbed that she was crying hysterically. It seemed to be par for the course, anymore. She was really such a drama queen at times. I figured she probably was crying because she got on the scale and found out her weight was higher than 120 lbs or something of the sort.

She shook her head. "I can't. I just can't say it. It's too horrible. It's just too horrible."

I sighed. I couldn't tell if she was doing her drama queen act or if something truly tragic had happened. "Please, Alexis, out with it."

"Ryan, it's about Mia."

I was startled. "What about her?" I suddenly realized the baby monitor was still on and I couldn't hear anything coming through it at all. "What about her?"

She shook her head. "I put her down around 8. Everything was fine. But I noticed around 10 that I didn't hear her anymore on the baby monitor. So I went in to look at her."

My heart suddenly was racing. Pounding, hard. I tried to imagine there wasn't anything wrong. That Mia was okay, but maybe there was an alarm that happened earlier, but it was a false alarm. It had to be something like that.

Fate wouldn't be that cruel. I hadn't had anything in my

life, ever, that made me happy the way Mia did. She had to be okay.

"Ryan, I don't know what happened. I don't know what happened."

"Where is Dana?" I asked. Dana wouldn't have let anything happen to Mia. Dana was always very diligent.

"I sent her home," she said. "She had to get home to attend to something happening with her mother."

My breathing started coming heavier. I looked at Alexis' eyes, and it was unmistakable. She was high. She was hysterical, but she was also unmistakably high. "Alexis, tell me what happened to Mia."

"I don't know," she said. "She just….stopped breathing."

I nodded. "She stopped breathing, but you caught it, and you were able to revive her, right? Right?"

She shook her head. "No, Ryan. I didn't catch it. I didn't catch it. I called Paul to come over and he did. He was here within minutes. I didn't know what to do, Ryan. I called Paul, and he tried to revive her, but she was…."

This wasn't happening. This was a nightmare. Mia wasn't dead. "I'm going in there," I said.

"You can't, Ryan. She's not there." She started crying again. "Paul called the coroner and they came and got her."

Coroner. Coroner. I couldn't grasp it. It was too horrible.

I ran up to Mia's room, and, as Alexis said, she wasn't in her crib. Now my heart was pounding out of my chest. I picked up one of her stuffed animals, and I smelled it. There was the familiar baby scent on the bear and I inhaled it.

And then the tears started coming. They started as a trickle, but I soon found that I was howling. Howling, like a wolf. I sat down on the floor, the stuffed bear in my arm, and I howled.

I didn't know how long I was there, but, by the time I got up off the floor, I was able to keep it together. I was going to have to be a man about this. As difficult as this was, I was going to have to stiffen my spine and do everything expected of me. That would mean that I couldn't show any more emotion. I was going to have to stuff down my feelings about losing my precious child, and I was going to have carry on. I was a man, goddammit, and I wasn't going to fall apart.

I stood up, and Alexis was standing in the doorway. "I'm so sorry, Ryan, I wish I knew what happened."

I wanted to rip into her about being high when she was watching Mia. I wanted to rip into her about her general lack of feeling for the beautiful child. I wanted to rip into her for so many different things. Things that went way back.

But I didn't. "Alexis, it wasn't your fault. Sometimes these things happen. Nobody knows why. It wasn't your fault." I knew, though, even as I said those words, that I didn't mean them. I felt, deep down, that Alexis really *was* at fault. If she wasn't high, then she would have been paying more attention to the baby monitor, and she could have heard the second Mia stopped breathing and done something about it.

I didn't want to pile on her, though. Besides, I was at a bar when Mia breathed her last. How was I any better than Alexis? I wasn't exactly being diligent myself.

Of course, I didn't know Dana had an emergency and had to go home. If I would have known that, I would have tried to make it home much earlier. I certainly wouldn't have trusted Alexis to be alone with Mia.

"Do you really mean that? You don't blame me for this happening?"

"No, I don't blame you."

I put my arms around her, and she wrapped her own arms around me. She sobbed for hours as I stroked her hair.

I was finally feeling something for Alexis. It might have been pity, but it was the first non-hostile feeling I had had for her since I couldn't remember when.

I tried to stifle my own tears as she kept crying in my arms. "Shhhh, Alexis, it's okay. Don't blame yourself. It's okay."

She shook her head. "No, Ryan, it's not okay. It will never be okay. We lost her. We lost her, Ryan. I'm not a mother anymore. And you're not a father."

Those words hit me in the heart like a dagger. I was no longer a father. I had just lost the light of my life. The one thing that had brought me out of the darkness that had always followed me. I thought Mia would be the thing that would make me want to keep going. To keep living.

Now she was gone.

And so was I.

Chapter Eleven

It was only a matter of time when Alexis managed to turn the entire thing back on me. In fact, it was less than 24 hours. She got her tears out of her system, and she came home after seeing one of her girlfriends for lunch to tear into me.

"I just had lunch with Roberta," she said to me. "I told her what happened. And she said this whole thing is your fault."

I drew a breath. I had spent most of the day doing nothing but staring at the wall. Nick had come over, and I finally was able to make funeral plans, with his help. He just came in and helped me take charge. I had an appointment set up with a funeral home, and he helped me make the phone calls to everyone.

I had no idea what I would do without that guy.

"How is this my fault?"

"You didn't let me breast feed. If you would have let me breast feed, our daughter would be alive today."

I sighed. "Yes, I know, Alexis. Breastfeeding does protect

against SIDS. But I had good reasons to make sure you didn't do that, and I'm sticking to them."

"I hate you, Ryan," she said. "You killed our daughter."

Those words struck me like daggers again. I was feeling, more and more, like my heart was literally breaking in two. Alexis' words weren't helping that at all. "Alexis, think what you want. I'm terribly sorry for the fact that I discouraged you from breastfeeding, but I couldn't let you go off your meds."

"Well, I did go off my meds," she said, and I wasn't at all surprised. "I went off my meds, because I was going to try to breastfeed her."

"I see," I said. "And this would be why you got back on your illegal drugs. And wouldn't this be the real reason you were never able to breastfeed Mia? Huh, Alexis? You certainly could never breastfeed her if you had heroin in your system, now could you?"

She shook her head. "I got back on the heroin because you rejected me, Ryan. I knew you wouldn't be on my side if I went off my meds, which is why I turned back to my old bad habits. If you just would have been reasonable, then we could have worked together. We could have worked together to make sure I could taper off the meds safely, and then I wouldn't have turned to the heroin and the cocaine, and I would have been able to breastfeed her. And she would be alive today."

I was astounded at her twisted logic, yet, at the same time, I strangely saw her point. "Alexis, I'm sorry. I'm sorry you blame me for this."

"I do. I do blame you for this. You're a bastard. If you weren't at the bar, then you would have been home, and you could have heard when Mia stopped breathing. And you would have been able to revive her. I don't know CPR. You do, though. You do, Ryan. So, there you go. You didn't let me breast feed, and you weren't home to deal with her. So, I do blame you, Ryan. I 100% blame you."

"Alexis, you aren't rational," I said calmly. "I didn't know Dana had gone home. If I did, I would have come home that instant. I checked my phone messages, Alexis, and there wasn't one message from you that said that you sent Dana home because of her emergency. So, I was unaware that Mia was alone with you."

"Well, you shouldn't have been drinking at that bar. You had a responsibility to this home, Ryan."

I drew a deep breath and tried, very hard, not to take her bait.

I tried, but I failed.

"Listen, Alexis, the reason why I was at this bar was because I didn't want to face you. You had me fucking thrown in jail on a pretense that I was abusing you. I wasn't abusing you and you know that. I simply wanted to see your arms and you refused. So, I had just spent two humiliating days in jail and going to court. And I knew just what your plan was, Alexis. You were trying to trap me into this marriage so I wouldn't leave. You knew that if I had an assault charge on my record that I probably couldn't get custody of Mia." I was ranting, and, by this point, I couldn't stop. "So, I had enough of your bullshit, Alexis. I had enough of your bullshit and I had to go to that bar to collect my thoughts about us."

"Oh, no," she said. "You aren't going to put this on me."

"You're a goddamned delusional bitch," I said. "If you think for one second that your manipulative ways were not the reason I wasn't home when my beautiful daughter breathed her last, then you need to see a fucking shrink.

You're the one who put bullshit charges on me because you wanted me to be trapped with you. Well, guess what? I'm not trapped with you anymore."

That woke her up. "What are you saying?"

"I'm saying it's time for me to get out of this toxic relationship. It's time for me to move on and find somebody who will actually make me happy. I loved Mia. I loved her more than I ever thought it was possible to love another human being. But she was the ONLY reason why I was with you, and now she's gone. And so will I be, soon."

She looked stricken. "You can't leave me, Ryan. You can't. You wouldn't be here if not for me. I got you out of your father's home, and I helped you get established with Nick. We've been together since we were 13 years old. You can't leave me, Ryan. You have to help me get through this. You have to help me. If you don't, then I'm going to spiral. I'm going to spiral, then I'm going to be in dangerous territory. I don't think you want that on your head."

I couldn't believe how manipulative she was. And I wasn't going to have it.

"Listen, Alexis, whatever is going to happen is going to happen. You've made your bed. I need to get away from you."

"Ryan, you can't just leave me."

I knew she was right. I needed to at least be there for her while she was grieving. If she was grieving for Mia. She was manipulative, but I was letting her be.

I'll only be in this house until she gets over this.

I was already looking forward to the day when I could leave. Because it was going to come one day.

Of that, I was sure.

Chapter Twelve

Sarah arrived the next day, having driven from her home on the Vineyard, her dog Coriolanus in tow. She got out of the car, and gave me a long hug. "Ryan, I'm so sorry," she said to me, tears in her eyes. "Peanut, my heart is breaking for you."

I nodded. "I'm really happy you're here," I said.

"Of course, I'm here. I was hoping that I could help you, uh, plan everything."

"It's going to be low-key," I said. "Just a few friends. I tried to contact our mom, but, of course, she can't get out of the institution. Which is tragic, because she met Mia, and she really loved her."

This was true. I took Mia to see her when Mia was a month old, and my mom really bonded with her. For Mia's part, it was strange, but she seemed very aware. She was only a month old, but she grabbed my mom's nose and gurgled. She almost seemed like she was pre-verbal, even as young as she was.

"Oh, I wish there was something I could say or do," she

said. "You've had just the shittiest life imaginable. Now this. I thought this would be the one thing that would really bring happiness to your life. It just doesn't seem fair."

I tousled her hair. "Sarah, I'm going to be okay. I know what you're thinking. You're thinking I'm going to go off the deep end and start using again. But I'm not. I'm substituting art for drugs. I've gotten back into painting and it's really helping me. It's taking my mind off my pain and I haven't had the urge to use at all."

Her face looked relieved. "Yes, I was worried about that," she said. "I've been worried about that ever since I heard you and Alexis got married. I know how awful the two of you are together."

"We are," I said. "But Mia made it all worth it. Mia made it worth it to be with her. We made a beautiful child. A beautiful child who was intelligent and docile and sweet." I didn't tell Sarah about Alexis and her trumped-up charges, or her accusations that I was at fault for Mia's death. Or, for that matter, about Alexis' recent return to illegal drugs.

I had made the decision, for now, to stay with Alexis, and I knew that if I told Sarah these things about Alexis, Sarah would be relentlessly on me to leave her. And I wanted to leave her. I did. But Alexis needed me. She needed me, and I was going to try to stick it out for now.

Sarah made a face. "I don't want to be blunt while you're grieving, but, Peanut, now that there isn't anything tying the two of you together, I hope you get out. Get out while you can."

"I'm going to," I said. "I'm going to, but I can't abandon her right now. She's grieving our child and she's using again. I need to make sure she gets help for her drug problems, and I have to make sure that she mentally doesn't completely break down because of this. So, I'm staying with her for the time being."

Sarah looked astounded. "You need to see somebody. You need to see somebody who can help you break ties with that witch. She's manipulating you. She's always manipulated you. She's still doing it, and Ryan, you need to see that about her. I know you always want to see the best in others, but there's no good in her. No good at all. You need to be happy, Ryan. You'll never be happy as long as Alexis is in your life."

I opened my mouth to protest, but nothing came out.

"I'm going to get out," I said. "But not right now. She needs me right now. If I leave her now, she'll probably end up killing herself. At the very least, she's going to be back in the mental hospital. I can't live with that. I know what you're saying, but I have to have some compassion with her. Deep down, there's a good person there. Underneath all the drug abuse and her mood disorder, there's a wonderful woman. She's sick, Sarah. She's sick, and I can't leave her, anymore than I would leave her if she had something like cancer or another disease such as this."

Sarah shook her head. "I don't believe you. You're sacrificing your happiness again, and for what? What has she ever done for you?"

"She saved my life," I said. "She was the one who convinced Nick to take me in all those years ago. Without her…"

"Without Nick, you mean," Sarah said. "Nick was one who took you in when you needed a place to go. Not Alexis. Alexis has been nothing but poison for you. She makes me sick. She's the reason why you turned to drugs. Her. She's ruined your life, and you continue to let her do it."

I knew Sarah was 100% right, but, at the same time, I

knew I didn't want to hear it. Because I was going to stay with Alexis, at least until I thought Alexis was out of the woods. "Alexis is my wife," I said to Sarah. I tried hard to sound more confident in my words than I felt. "Like it or not, she's my wife. And I need to stand by her. At least for now."

Sarah sighed. "Peanut, I want you to come home with me. Stay with Gil and me for a little while. Get your head together. Meet some people. Some good people. Don't get me wrong, you have Nick in your life, and he's probably the most positive thing you got. But you seem to be under Alexis' spell, and I don't think Nick is strong enough to get you to break it. You need a change of scenery. Come and stay with us."

I nodded my head. "Good people. You mean good women, don't you? You want to interfere with my life, still. Now who's being manipulative?"

"Yes, I mean women," she said. "I have so many girl-friends who would love a guy like you. You have so much going for you. I don't think you see that, but I do. You need to be with somebody who's going to appreciate you and what you have to offer. And that person isn't Alexis."

"Oh, okay. Okay. I guess I'll just leave my job and go and play with you and your silly girlfriends on the Vineyard. Then I'll come back here to Kansas City to a dead wife and no job. Because I will lose my job if I take an extended leave and Alexis won't make it without me. She's fragile and I need to be here to make sure she doesn't end it all."

"You're getting defensive," she said to me. "I hope you're keeping up with your therapy with Dr. Halder. And I hope you're being honest with him about what's going on with you and Alexis. Because you need to hear the truth from him. He'll tell you to get the hell out while you can."

"Of course I'm keeping up my therapy with Dr. Halder," I said. "Listen, Sarah, we need to drop this subject. I'm going to stay with Alexis, at least until I know she won't fall apart if I leave, and that's that. I need to think about burying my beautiful daughter. That's all that's important right now. That's all I should be thinking about. That's all you should be helping me with. Maybe Alexis and I will get a divorce in the near future. Maybe not. But that can't be my prime concern right now. And it shouldn't be yours, either."

Sarah finally looked defeated. "I know. I know, Peanut. I'm sorry. She just pisses me off so much, you just can't even imagine. I hate her."

"Duly noted," I said. "And I've heard that from you ever since Alexis and I got together. So you're saying nothing new."

"Well, let me just say this, and then, you're right, we need to focus on Mia. She's what's most important. But I will tell you that I hate Alexis because I blame her for all the bad things that have happened to you in your life. You wouldn't have been on drugs if it weren't for her. She has never cared about you. I have never understood why a handsome, intelligent and caring man like you could be with a narcissist like her for even two seconds. You can do so much better. So much better."

I rolled my eyes. I had heard this speech so many fucking times....and I knew she was partially wrong. Alexis *wasn't* the proximate cause for my drug use. My fucked-up life was the proximate cause for my drug use. There was something buried deep in my subconscious that had always caused me to want to die. And to use. I didn't know what it was, but it was there, right on the surface. Alexis had alluded to it several times. I didn't want to know what it was, though. All I knew was that if I didn't have a fucked-up life, I would've been normal. Alexis or no, I would've been normal.

But I wasn't normal. I was messed up.

And Alexis had nothing to do with that.

FOR SARAH'S PART, SHE WAS AS GOOD AS HER WORD. She said her piece, and then she and I did what we had to do to make sure Mia's service was beautiful. And she helped me get through it in one piece.

It was hardest thing I did – getting it all together. Alexis wasn't helping me. She had long since retired to her bedroom. I sent Nick in there to talk to her, and make sure she didn't go too much over the edge, and he, surprisingly, had no qualms about doing that for me.

So Sarah and I did all the preparation. I chose Mia's clothing and I picked out a little casket for her. I wanted to break down, every minute of every day, but I kept it together.

I had to get through these next few days – the guests, the service, all of that – and then I could break down. I gave myself that permission to not try to be so strong after all the preparations were put into place.

THE DAY OF THE SERVICE WAS FINALLY UPON ME. I got Nick to get Alexis out of her bedroom and make sure she was coherent for the service. I knew she had to be there. She had to have that chance to say goodbye to our daughter.

So I went with Sarah to the church. Nick and Alexis followed closely behind in Nick's car.

The service was well-attended. There wasn't a eulogy. I

didn't really know what to say. She was only a baby. I didn't think it was necessarily appropriate for there to be one. And Alexis was in no shape to address the people who came to pay their respects.

Afterwards, we all met at my house and I had a spread catered in for everyone. I put on my happy face and greeted everyone who came in. There were plenty of hugs, plenty of tears. Plenty of people who came up with the usual clichés about God needing an angel and about how God works in mysterious ways.

I bit my tongue, of course, because I knew these people meant well. They didn't know what else to say. So I nodded whenever somebody came up to me to tell me about how God called Mia home because He was short of angels.

Alexis, however, wasn't so circumspect. "Don't tell me that bullshit," I heard her tell an elderly woman who apparently told Alexis the same thing she told me. "Goddamn, you people are all the same. All this crap about it being God's will and all of that bullshit. If you really think God is cruel enough to take my little daughter before she ever had a chance to live, then what can I say? Your God is an asshole. There, I said it. He's an asshole. Why would he take Mia and leave all these future psychopaths on the earth? Tell me that!"

I silently applauded her stance. I wasn't going to say it. But I was certainly thinking it. It was like when people say their prayers were answered because their kid recovered. Which is to say that God plays favorites, because there were plenty of other children who don't survive their illnesses.

The old lady just shook her head. "I was trying to help."

"Well, that's not helping," Alexis raged. "It's not helping at all."

For a second, I thought Alexis was going to throw the

poor old woman out of the house, so I went over to Alexis and put my arm around her. "Alexis, have some empathy for these people. They literally don't have anything else to say but the usual clichés. They don't mean any harm for any of the things they're telling us."

But Alexis was not to be deterred. Nick had assured me that Alexis was sober, so this anger and rage was from something other than drugs. I wondered if she had spiraled into mania.

She violently shook her head. "I want her out of here. I want all of these people out of here. They don't know. They can't know. None of them have gone through what I've gone through. What we've gone through. They're looking at me like I'm some kind of charity case and I hate it. I hate being pitied, Ryan, and that's all I see is pity. Pity and goddamned bromides that are supposed to make me feel better but only makes me feel worse."

"Alexis, none of these people mean us any harm," I said. "They're just trying to pay their respect. We should let them."

"No," she said. "I won't stand here one more minute and let somebody tell me some more bullshit about God's will. I won't. You can if you want to, Ryan. But I'm going up to my room."

At that, she stormed up to her room, slamming the door behind her.

Sarah came up to me, putting her arm around me. "How are you holding up, Peanut?" she asked me. "I can tell how your wife is holding up," she said with a suppressed smile. "But how about you?"

I shook my head. "I don't know how I feel. I'm trying hard not to feel anything at all. If I let my guard down, the dam might break, and then I don't know what will happen.

I'm afraid to let that dam break. So I'm trying to avoid my feelings on this."

"Keep going to your therapy," she said. "Keep going, and maybe find a support group for you and Alexis to attend. Be around people who know what you're going through, because they've been there, too. That's really the best thing you can do right now. And allow yourself to feel."

I shook my head. Allowing myself to feel was dangerous at this point. I had gone through so much and there was even more that was buried. Excavating it at that moment could be beyond devastating. "I'm going to be okay, Sarah," I said. "I've been painting pictures of Mia these past few days. It's really helped."

She sighed. "I wish you would take me up on my offer to stay with me at the Vineyard," she said. "You know we have plenty of room and my kids adore you. They miss you."

I wanted to ask her where the kids were at that very moment, but I thought this question would inevitably come out more pointed than I meant it, so I bit my tongue and said nothing. "I know. I miss Alice and Henry too."

I mingled with the guests for the rest of the reception. And, after everyone had left, Sarah, Nick and I went out on my back patio and we all had a glass of wine.

Nick put his arm around me. "Man, this is a tough break, I know."

I nodded. Nick *did* know what it felt like to have a light go out, having lost his own daughter, tragically, some two years before. "I know. Thanks for being there. And thanks for taking over Alexis duty. It can't be easy dealing with her right now."

"She's not so bad," he said. "I mean, she is. But I my heart goes out to her. There's nothing more devastating than losing a child. I have my issues with her, same as everyone else, but she is really hurting."

Sarah said nothing, but just continued to sip her wine.

"Go ahead," I said to Sarah. "Say what you want to say about Alexis."

She shrugged. "You know how I feel about her. But Nick is right. She's going through something that no woman ever should. Or man, I might add." She put her arm around me. "I wish you could properly grieve. I'm worried that you're so closed off about all of this."

"I know, Sarah. But…." I trailed off. "There's something in my psyche. Something that's black and haunted. I'm afraid that if I really try to examine how I'm feeling about Mia that I'm going to excavate this other thing. And I literally don't know where I would be if that happened. So I think I need to leave well enough alone."

Sarah and Nick exchanged glances when I said that. And then Nick shook his head as if to say *not now. We can't talk to him about this now.*

"Well," Sarah said. "It's just as well, I guess, that you keep all your darkness buried. I'm afraid it's going to come out, though, and I'm afraid for what might happen when it does."

I knew Sarah and Nick knew things my conscious mind didn't. I could see it in their eyes. But I still wasn't in any shape to face them, especially right at that moment, so I decided to change the subject.

"Sarah," I said to her. "How did you feel when you first saw Gil?"

She shrugged. "I thought he was interesting. Then I got to know him and started to like his quirkiness. Why?"

I stared at my wine glass and the redhead popped into my mind. "But wasn't there somebody in your life where you felt drawn to him on first sight? I seem to remember that."

"Of course," she said. "Robert Carrington." She shook her head. "Oh my God. I saw him in a crowd, and my heart started beating out of my chest. I finally met him and talked to him, and it was like I was talking to a childhood friend. I've never had that reaction to anyone before or since."

"Robert Carrington," I said. "And what happened with him?"

"You know what happened with him," she said. "He was married when I met him, and we had that torrid affair where we couldn't keep our hands off each other. Then his wife found out about us and threatened to take his children away from him for good, so he broke it off with me." She shook her head. "But that was the only time where I was with a man where I felt like my core was truly shaken." She looked at me suspiciously. "Why do you ask?"

I shrugged. "No reason. I was just wondering if you have ever had that kind of feeling about somebody."

Nick was sitting next to me, and he shook his head as he drank his wine. "Ryan here thinks he's seen his soul mate," he said, as he made air quotes around the words "soul mate." "She's this dumpy little redheaded woman who could be considered cute if you're being charitable. Not his type at all."

I sat up straighter in my chair.

Sarah started laughing. "Peanut, is this true? Have you seen somebody who you feel is meant for you?"

I shrugged. "No. I mean, it's stupid. I don't really believe in all that soul mate crap and all of that." Even as I said those words, though, I realized that a part of me clearly did believe in the "soul mate crap." I shrugged again. "I don't know, I've just seen her around, everywhere I go, and there's something about her. That's all."

She nudged me. "Well, go for it. Life is too short to be with somebody who's wrong for you. Especially if you already know that somebody else is right for you."

I smiled. "I know you're right," I said.

Then I made a decision.

I was going to try to find her and see if there was something there.

At this point, I had nothing to lose.

Chapter Thirteen

The next day, even though I was still committed to staying with Alexis until I knew that she would be okay, I decided to try to take fate by the horns. There was something about that woman, and I hadn't been able to get her out of my mind. So, I was going to go to where she worked and try to meet her.

So, I headed downtown. I heard her tell her client that she was from the public defender's office, so I decided to head there first. And I heard her say her full name to that client - Iris Snowe. So, I had something to go on.

The public defender's office was located in an old white building that was around twenty stories tall. The elevator was slow, and the carpeting in the lobby, if you could call it that, was worn and thread-bare.

As I headed up, I had no idea what I was going to say. Could I say that I needed a public defender? That would seem silly. But I had to make up something.

What I didn't anticipate was that I would get to the suite where the Public Defender's office was and not see a receptionist. I was expecting that there would be somebody there to greet me, but there wasn't. There were people milling about, but there wasn't anybody who was just there to help me.

I felt embarrassed, but I was going to have to at least try.

I caught the eye of a tall blonde woman who stopped and looked at me awkwardly standing there. "May I help you?" she asked me. I knew by the look in her eyes that she realized that I probably wasn't a broke criminal in need of this office's services.

I don't know why I felt completely embarrassed, but I did. "Yes, hello, I'm looking for an attorney who works here. Her name is Iris Snowe."

The blonde nodded. "She doesn't work here anymore."

I gulped. I knew it wouldn't be as easy as just waltzing on into the Public Defender's office and asking for Iris. There always had to be complications. "Oh, okay," I said. "Could you give me information about where she's working now?"

"I'm sorry, it's the policy of this office not to give out that information. For obvious reasons."

I didn't know what the "obvious reasons" were, but I would imagine that it would have something to do with the nature of what this office did. They probably had problems with stalkers.

I was going to have to go to Plan B. Whatever that was.

I couldn't believe that I showed up at this place without a good plan for how I was going to meet this girl. I had to admit I did it on a whim, but I had to think on my feet. "I understand, but I'm not a client. I'm a process server. I met her a few months ago and she gave me her card. I'm interested in doing business with her."

The blonde looked me up and down, obviously

surmising that I probably was telling the truth about not being a client. "Well, I believe you," she said. "But I don't believe that we even have information about where she's practicing now."

I knew she was lying about that. I would imagine that former Public Defenders had to leave information about their next job, just in case the PDs office needed to get ahold of them to obtain some kind of information about their cases.

"Well," I began, and then I saw that Nick was calling me. For some odd reason, this startled me – mainly because Nick didn't generally call me during the day. "If you would excuse me," I said to the blonde girl. "I'll be right back."

She shook her head and said nothing, but just walked away.

"Yeah," I said to Nick.

"Ryan, there's a problem with Alexis."

"No shit," I said. "There's always a problem with her."

"No, really," he said. "She overdosed. She's at the hospital."

"Which hospital?" I asked. I should have been more concerned, but I had been through this so many times, it was like a drill anymore.

"St. Joseph's," he said. "This is different than the other times, Ryan."

"Oh? How is it different?"

"This time it was deliberate."

Chapter Fourteen

I sighed. "Deliberate. And what makes you think that?"

"Because it wasn't illegal drugs this time. It was sleeping pills. She took the entire bottle."

"I better get down there," I said.

The Public Defender's office was going to have to wait. That was just as well. If I walked away at that moment, I could have some time to think about how to get the information that I needed about this Iris person.

As I headed back to my car, I thought about if I needed to be worried about Alexis. This was apparently a suicide attempt, and she hadn't actually attempted suicide before. So, this was different than all the other overdoses she had experienced in the past.

Alexis was addicted, depressed and, sometimes, psychotic. But she hadn't actually been actively suicidal thus far.

At the same time, I was tired. I was worn out. What happened with Mia sapped any kind of energy I had for life. I hadn't recovered from that in the least. I hadn't even started the grieving process for my beautiful little girl. So, there was a part of me that was numb. Numb to Alexis' suffering. Numb to just about anything around me.

She was like the little girl who cried wolf to me at this point. I had gone round and round and round with her and I just wanted off the ride.

However, when I got to the hospital, and went into her room, I changed my mind. She was glassy eyed and looked so lost. She had definitely hit bottom at that point, from what I could see.

In spite of myself, my heart went out to her.

"Ryan," she said softly. "I can't believe you came."

"Of course," I said. "What kind of a monster would I be if I stayed away when you really needed me?"

"Dana called Nick," she said. "I'm so sorry she didn't call you. She panicked and called the first number she saw, and that was Nick's number on the refrigerator. I don't think she remembered your number. I asked her to input all of our numbers on her phone, but I guess she didn't get around to it."

"I understand," I said. I was wondering why Nick was called and not me, but that concern was not first on my mind at that point.

I gently brushed some of her hair off her face. I kissed her forehead and wondered if this would be the incident that would finally bring us together. Seeing her like this touched my heart in a way that I hadn't quite expected. She wasn't the hard Alexis that I had come to see all these years. That façade had been stripped away, and the woman in that bed looked softer. Vulnerable. Sad and lost.

She started to cry. "Oh, Ryan, I'm so sorry I did this. I know you probably thought I didn't really care about Mia because of the way I acted. But I did, Ryan. I loved her very much. I was just so depressed, I couldn't see straight. And I know you tried to help me and I love you for that. Now she's gone, Ryan. She's gone, and I feel like I don't have anything at all anymore."

I squeezed her hand. "I know, Alexis. I know you're grieving. I know you loved her."

She turned her head to look out the window. "And, Ryan, I know that you've heard this from me all of our lives together, but I want to change. I need to change. Please, Ryan, I know we haven't always gotten along, but I want all that to change. I'll do anything you ask of me. I'll go into rehab, I'll get my meds adjusted. I'll go to counseling. Just please don't leave me."

I drew a breath. At the moment, she looked completely sincere. I had misgivings about giving her another chance, of course, but there was something in her eyes that made actually want to give her a chance. A real chance.

"Alexis, we'll talk about this when you recover."

"No, Ryan," she said with tears in her eyes. "I need to talk about this now. I need to know that you'll be there for me when I get out. Otherwise, I'll just sit here in this bed and obsess and lose my will to live."

I took her hand and kissed it softly. "Of course I'll be there," I found myself saying. "We're going through this loss together. We need to be strong for each other and help each other through. So, yes, Alexis, I'll be there. I do love you."

She smiled and started to laugh. "Oh, thank God. I was so afraid...."

She didn't finish that thought. But she didn't really have to. I knew what she was going to say. She was afraid that I was going to leave her now that we didn't have a real reason to try to stay together. Then she would have nothing.

"Shhhh, Alexis, you don't have to be afraid. I know that

we haven't always gotten along, but I also know that, under-neath it all, there's a beautiful person in there. I know how much you've been hurt by your family, and by my father. You're scared and lonely, and sometimes you act out. But I think that we can try to get past all of that. Try to get past all of the hurt and pain we've caused each other and try to find something real."

I realized as I said those words that I meant them. I suddenly remembered what it was about Alexis that made me fall in love with her in the first place – that she really wasn't a bad person. She was scarred and often had up her walls, but, if you get past all of that, there was a sweet person who was wanting to emerge.

"Thank you, Ryan. Thank you for giving me hope." She shook her head. "I was just laying here before you came in, thinking the worst. I was thinking that I not only lost my baby, but that I lost you, too. Thank you for giving me another chance. And I promise that I'll be good. I'll do everything that you ask of me."

I nodded. There was a voice inside of me that was screaming that Alexis was going to go back to her old tricks. And that she would never change. Could ever really change.

But I ignored that voice and said to her "I know you will."

And that was that.

We were back together for real.

Chapter Fifteen

Alexis got out of the hospital after five days, and I made it a point to see her every single day in the hospital. We were back to how we used to be, when things were good – we were laughing again and talking like friends. I even climbed into her bed one evening and we watched reality television and made fun of the people on there. Reality television was never my thing, but Alexis loved it. But I could make her laugh with my comments about the characters I saw on those shows.

"Stop, Ryan, please," she said as she doubled over with laughter at something I said about the Real Housewives of whatever. "I can't breathe."

I was laughing, too. It seemed wonderful. Like old times. When times were good, that is. My mind focused on that – on the good times we had shared. I tried not to think about all the bad shit that went down between us.

"Well, let's see...maybe we can find a Jerry Springer rerun and then I can really let it rip."

Alexis wasn't laughing anymore, but she put her head

on my shoulder. She seemed to be such a little girl when she did that. "I love this," she said. "It seems so silly, just sitting here and watching these stupid shows with you. But it reminds me of when I was a young girl and watching a beauty pageant with my mom on a Saturday night. We always used to make comments about the girls, just like you are with these real housewives."

I chuckled. "You know these housewives aren't real, don't you? God forbid actual housewives act like these women. And some of them aren't even wives at all. What's up with that? And that term, housewives. That sounds so dated and politically incorrect."

"I know. But it's fun to watch them, isn't it?"

"Sure. And tonight we watch The Bachelor." I started laughing. "And I know how much you love that show. Even if the couple ends up breaking up after a week or so after the show ends."

"Nuh uh," she said. "They've been getting married lately. So there."

"Well, maybe true love can be found by dating 25 women and sleeping with three of them." I shook my head. "That wouldn't be my way of going about it, but to each his own."

She looked up at me, her blue eyes shining. "How is true love found in your world, Ryan?" she asked hopefully. "Maybe true love can come with somebody who you've known most of your life and who really loves you."

I sighed and held her tighter. "One step at a time, Alexis. You stay on your meds and stay away from using, and maybe things will fall into place. But the ball is in your court."

"I know, Ryan," she said. "And you'll see after I get out of this place. The doctors have adjusted my meds and I'm feeling better than I have for a long time. I think I really went through a dark period after Mia was born, because my hormones weren't right. My doctor told me that, because I have a pre-existing mood disorder, I'm more prone to post-partum depression than most other women. But things are definitely getting better for me."

"I know you are. You look better than you've looked in a long time." I didn't want to say, though, what was on my mind – that she looked so unhappy when Mia was alive, and now she looked...relaxed. Less stressed. Lighter. She was wearing no makeup, but she was positively glowing.

I didn't want to acknowledge that maybe Mia was the cause of her distress. And now that she was gone....I shook my head. Alexis was grieving Mia, I knew that. Yet I couldn't escape the fact that she seemed like a great burden had been lifted from her.

Then again, Alexis did have a meds adjustment and I knew, from looking in her eyes, that she hadn't been using. So that might be the real reason why she seemed so much happier now than before.

At least I hoped that was the reason.

THE FIVE DAYS FINALLY WERE UP. Alexis was feeling better and she was going to leave the hospital. And it was time for our "exit interview," which is what patients have to do before they get out of the hospital. The doctor would go over the new meds protocol and what was expected of Alexis and of me, as I was going to be her designated "caretaker."

The doctor sat us down and explained that he took Alexis off of some of her meds and put her on different ones. He explained the dosage and when she would be expected to take these meds. He also went over what else was expected of us, as far as the fact that Alexis was required to complete outpatient group counseling for a six-month period. I also was advised on what to look for to make sure that Alexis was recovering, and how to tell if she was on the verge of another breakdown.

I smiled politely, but I knew all of this. I knew Alexis better than she knew herself. And I knew all the signs that she was about to go Defcon One or when she was using. I regretted not getting Alexis help earlier when she started to isolate, but I thought she just needed space and she would come out of it.

I made a silent vow not to be that naïve again.

"Thank you, Dr. Brack," I said to him. "I'll make sure Alexis stays on her meds and I'll go to her counseling sessions with her."

Dr. Brack nodded and shook my hand. "Good luck to you," he said to me. "And you, Alexis."

She smiled and shook his hand. "Thanks for everything."

And the two of us walked, hand in hand, out the door of the hospital.

We got in my car. "Okay, Alexis, where to? I think we should probably go out to eat tonight. What do you think about that?"

Alexis was quiet. "Sure," she said without enthusiasm.

I grabbed her hand. "What's wrong?" I asked.

"Oh, nothing," she said, but then started to cry. "I'm just afraid, that's all. I'm back in the real world, and I have to go home where…." Then she really started to sob. "Oh, God, Ryan, I don't know if I can face it. When I was in the hospital, everything seemed to be okay. I was safe. I didn't even think about Mia the whole time I was there. I was only focused on my recovery. Now, I have to face it."

And, just like that, I saw the real reason why Alexis seemed so relaxed and happy in the hospital. She wasn't living in the real world in the hospital. And now she was going to have to go home to a place that seemed to be haunted.

"Alexis," I said to her. "Maybe we should move."

She shook her head. "No, Ryan. I can't bear to move her things. To disturb her room in any way. I hope you understand. I probably will be ready to do all of that in the future, but I just don't feel strong enough to do that." She looked panicked that I would even suggest moving. "I can't face it, Ryan, please."

"Relax, Alexis," I said, taking her hand and bringing it to my mouth. "It was only a suggestion. I thought it would be a good one."

"Why? Do you think we should move on? Pretend she never existed?"

"No," I said. "That wasn't what I was thinking at all. I just thought…"

"Thought what? That moving into a new place would just erase her from our memories?" Now she was getting agitated. "How can you even think that, Ryan?"

I sighed. "I wasn't thinking that, Alexis. Please don't put words in my mouth." I wondered if the peace I experienced with her in the hospital was all a mirage. I wondered, again, if I was making a mistake by staying with her.

She calmed down. "I'm sorry," she said. "I'm just very sensitive. My emotions are difficult for me to control. And I'm so apprehensive about going home. I don't want to face the memories there. Not just the memories of Mia, but me.

How I was. I'm so afraid the house has picked up all of my negative energy and it's going to put it back on me."

"Alexis, that's silly. Negative energy isn't going to stay in that house."

"I think it will. Ryan, have you ever been in a house where something just doesn't seem right? I mean, it might be a gorgeous home with all new furnishing and everything is in place, but you walk in, and it's just oppressive? There's something in the air?"

I thought about what she was saying and I knew she was right. I *did* feel that way when I walked into a house one time. It was a beautiful Tudor-style home in an upscale neighborhood, and the inside was gorgeous. Yet, I felt a heaviness in that home. I couldn't place it, but I wanted to get out of that place the second I went into it.

I later on found the woman living there was suffering through terrible depression. But I didn't really put that together with why I felt like the house was foreboding.

"Alexis, it's going to be okay," I said. "The house isn't threatening. It's not depressed. It's an inanimate object – it can't get depressed. So, relax, please." I took her hand. "Everything will be okay."

She looked out the window. "Can we have Nick over tonight?"

I raised my eyebrows. "That was out of the blue," I said. "Why do you want to see him?"

She sighed. "I just want company, Ryan. Somebody who isn't grieving. I need to be around somebody who hasn't just suffered a traumatic loss. Do you think he can come over?"

"I'm sure he would be able to," I said. I wanted to ask her if her stated reasons were the real reasons she wanted Nick over, or if she actually wanted to make a play for him, but I held my tongue.

Ryan, if this is going to work between the two of you, you need to learn to trust her.

"Thanks, Ryan," she said. "See if he wants to come over for dinner. Without Rielle."

I smiled. Neither of us liked the snooty woman Nick was married to. I, personally, couldn't see why he was with her. But, then again, he couldn't ever see why I was with Alexis, so who was I to judge?

"Okay," I said. "I'll give him a call."

"Now?"

"Okay, yes, now," I said, and I dialed him on my satellite phone attached to my car.

He answered the phone. "Hey, what's up?"

"Nick, can you come over tonight? Alexis is getting out of the hospital and she wants a little intimate house-warming party."

"Sure," he said. "What time?"

"How about 7? I can make dinner for the three of us."

"I'm there," he said. "See you then."

I looked over at Alexis, and she had a faint smile on her face. "Thank you for doing that," she said.

"Of course," I said. "I don't mind having Nick over at all. I never do."

She nodded her head. "I hope you don't think I don't want to be alone with you. I mean, I don't right now. But we're in such a bad place right now, both of us. I mean, you don't show it, but I know you feel as badly as I do about Mia. You're just stronger than me, so you don't show it as much."

I wanted to tell her the truth. That my heart was torn apart. Absolutely ripped out of my body. That I went home every night after seeing her in the hospital and cried in Mia's room. I never wanted to show Alexis that, though. I had to be strong for her. If I showed Alexis how I was really feeling about losing my daughter, than I couldn't do what I needed to do to make sure she recovered from it.

"I miss her, Alexis. I do."

She got quiet. "Mia was the only thing in your life that was pure, wasn't she? You've gone through so much and I've put you through so much, too. And I think you were finally happy when Mia was born. I'm so sorry about that, Ryan."

I cleared my throat, because there was a lump forming there. I blinked back tears. "You know me so well, Alexis. We might not always get along, but you do know me."

And that was really all that I could ask for at that moment – to be with a woman who really knew me. All my darkness, my past, the things I did – she knew about all of them.

That would have to be enough.

Chapter Sixteen

IRIS

After the Michael disaster, I found myself isolating more and more. I had no idea when I was going to finally meet the guy who was for me. Michael replied to an email that I sent him about our meeting, saying that he pretty much only dates "stunning" women. I guess I wasn't stunning enough for him. I really thought that his ex-girlfriend Kiera wasn't stunning, anyhow. She looked like the generic bleached blonde who wore way too much makeup and starved herself. I went to the University of Missouri, and women like Kiera were a dime a dozen in the sorority houses. Ninety percent of the women in the Delta Gamma house looked like her. It wasn't like she was a supermodel or something – she was merely pretty, but who knows what she looked like under all that paint?

I was beginning to think, though, that men didn't go for women like me. I didn't bleach my hair, I didn't wear a shit-ton of makeup, and I had a very healthy appetite. Too healthy, unfortunately, as I was constantly battling my weight. At the moment, I was at my heaviest, and I wasn't happy about that. It wasn't like I didn't try to maintain my weight, though. I did – I tried Keto, Nutri-System and Weight Watchers. I would lose the weight, then lose focus, and it would come right back on.

But I did have something to look forward to that evening – dinner with my best girlfriend, Debbie. We were going to have drinks and dinner. I really needed to bounce some ideas off her, because I was in transition, having finally left my job at the Public Defender's office and I was in private practice. Which wasn't going well – I found that I had to get clients, and I really had no idea how to do that. I rented space in a suite that had other lawyers, and, at the moment, I was making money covering for them in different courts. But that wasn't exactly a good way to make enough money to live, and I was living off my meager savings that soon would dry up.

I got some referrals, too, from the guys in my office, which meant I got my first retainer for a divorce. But I couldn't touch that money until I actually did work for the client, so that money was in trust, and, therefore, didn't help me.

The upshot was that I was broke and lonely. And I had no idea how I was going to change that. So, I got lost in *Sex and the City* on Max, binge-watching it just about every night in my tiny apartment with my cat.

This was really no way to live.

I MET DEBBIE AT 7 THAT EVENING. We were having dinner at the Olive Garden by my house. I knew this wasn't really Italian food, any more than On the Border was Mexican food, but it was comforting and it reminded me of my family. This was always our place to eat whenever somebody in my family had a birthday. And I did love the salad and breadsticks.

I sat down. She was already there. "Sorry I'm late," I said. I didn't try to make an excuse for why I was late, because I really didn't have one. I simply got wrapped up in a show that I was watching, and I lost track of time.

"Don't worry about it," she said. "I'm really happy to see you. How are things?"

"They're okay. I'm really questioning my decision to go out on my own. I mean, I wasn't happy at the Public Defender's Office, but at least I was getting a steady paycheck. As miniscule as it was."

She nodded her head. "Well, try not to worry. You'll get clients coming in sooner or later."

"I know." I felt a lump in my throat. She was recently married and had a baby on the way. I tried to tamp down my feelings of envy about that. After all, she had gone through quite a bit in her own life. She deserved every bit of happiness.

So did I, though. When would I get my chance?

"So, what else is going on? How is the dating scene?"

I shrugged my shoulders. "What dating scene? God, it seems that the only guys I meet anymore are total losers. Well, not losers, but not for me. Or I'm not for them. But, who knows? There was this guy that I met the other night. No chemistry, but he has been calling. Maybe I'll give him more of a shot."

"That sounds promising," she said. "You should give him a shot, even if you're not feeling it. Sometimes you can start to feel it after a little bit. You would be surprised."

I nodded, not convinced. I remembered earlier on in my dating life, and I went out with this guy. And all that I could think was that I really wanted to stay home with my roommates and watch a movie. They were getting ready to pop in a movie, and they had popcorn popped, and, the entire time I was out with this guy, I thought about how much I should have stayed home.

This guy who was calling me made me feel like that. When I was on my date with him, all I could think about was that I wanted to go home and hang out with my cat.

But, still, there wasn't anything necessarily wrong with him. Maybe he was a diamond in the rough.

Debbie put her hand on my hand. "You've really had a tough time since Travis, haven't you?"

"No, no," I said. "That was so long ago." And it *was* a long time ago. For a long time, I was a basket case over him and the way that he treated me. Basically, we lived together, and he and I spent the holidays with his toxic parents back east. He had told me, prior to taking me to meet them, that he had wanted to marry me, but I needed to meet his mother first. Naturally, I thought this trip back east was the final step he needed to take and that he and I soon would be engaged.

So, I suffered through the week with his mom and dad. I had met his father, who was a complete racist bastard. His father used the "n" word in casual conversation, and, when he met me, he only had one thing to say to Travis – that he thought I would be thinner.

I wasn't looking forward to spending the entire week with his father, but I hoped his mother would redeem the whole thing.

She didn't. A former beauty queen, she was tall and lean and probably the most snobbish woman I'd ever met. It also didn't help that she was running a high fever, as she was very sick that week. Still, she did everything that week in preparations for Christmas. Travis's father didn't lift a finger, and even had the nerve to ask his mother to get him another piece of pie while he sat in his chair.

Add in Travis' sister, whom he hated, so he refused to even say hello to her when she came to visit. Which made his father lose his temper and scream and yell at him right in front of everybody. We hightailed it out of there during his father's rant, without even saying goodbye to everyone.

In all, it was a sacrifice for me to spend the holidays there. I missed my own family, for our Christmases were always warm and happy. But I thought it was necessary. I wanted to marry Travis, and, now that I met his mother, I thought the last hurdle had been knocked down.

So, imagine my shock when, two days after we got back from the visit to his parents, he sat me down and told me he wanted me to move out.

"I just need space," he had said. "I still want to be with you, but maybe we need to just not live together anymore. We can still date."

I was naïve. I took him at his word – that he and I were still together, but we were just not going to live together under the same roof. I cried a million tears that week, as I found a new place to live, but I told myself that it was all temporary. He would come to his senses and we would still end up getting married.

That didn't happen, of course. I went through the worst depression of my life in the wake of my abruptly being asked to leave our home. And, six months after I moved out, I found out everything that had happened. About exactly why he had changed his mind about me.

Turns out that he had met somebody one month before I went back east to meet his parents. He called her every day while he was seeing his parents, apparently when I wasn't paying attention.

Come to think of it, there were many times when he had locked himself in his room, giving me some excuse that I bought.

I got a phone call from this woman, as she proceeded to tell me that she had dumped him, and then she laid everything on me. When they met, when they first had sex – which was when he was still with me – and the first time that he told her he loved her. Also when he was still with me.

I felt stupid at that time. All that time, I thought he would come back to me. The thought that he had met somebody else never even crossed my mind.

Ironically, I bonded with this woman, whose name was Gretchen. We talked for hours, laughing about how Travis used the exact same lines on both of us. Talking to her actually helped me heal from my broken heart.

I was completely hurt, though, and my self-esteem felt like it was trampled. I had no idea why I wasn't good enough, and, when Gretchen told me how Travis bad-mouthed me to her, my blood boiled. I did everything for this guy, and I put up with him screaming and yelling at me for tiny little things. And he was probably the laziest guy I had ever known. He never did dishes, never vacuumed, never did laundry, never cooked, never went to the store, and he left his t-shirts on the floor for me to pick up. When his father came to visit, I spent eight hours getting the place clean. He didn't lift a finger to help, even though it was *his* father visiting.

I did all of this without complaint, even though both of us were working full time. Then he dumped me, not even respecting me enough to tell me the actual reason why.

Unfortunately, this was my only real relationship that I had in my life. After he dumped me, I licked my wounds for several years before deciding to get on the Internet dating roller coaster.

And, thus far, the Internet dating roller coaster was a disaster.

"I know it's been several years," she said. "But maybe you have a wall up. He really screwed you over. You might not even realize you have a wall up." She dug into her salad, which had just arrived at the table, dipping her bread stick into the little dish of ranch dressing that accompanied the salad at our request. "Maybe you should see somebody."

"Maybe," I said. "When I get insurance, I'll think about seeing a therapist about all of that. You might be right. I might just be scared of getting hurt again, so I'm subconsciously picking losers or guys that aren't interested in me." I smiled. "In the meantime, I have my pit bulls. I am so in love with these dogs, and they really give me a sense of purpose." I shrugged. "Maybe that's all that I'll ever have is the unconditional love of these precious animals."

I didn't want to believe that, though. I wanted to believe my heart was open and I was ready to receive the love I deserved. The alternative would be that I would always be alone, and that was something scarier to me than anything else.

She smiled. "You have a lot to offer somebody, you know."

"I know," I said, but I wasn't entirely convinced. Travis had made me feel worthless. I knew it wasn't fair – his issues were his own and really had nothing to do with me. But I couldn't shake the feeling that I just wasn't good enough for him. And if I wasn't good enough for a snake like that, maybe I wasn't good enough for anyone at all.

"Anyhow, why don't we catch a chick flick after this?" she said. "There are some good ones playing."

"That sounds like fun," I said. That was one thing that tended to cheer me up – watching mindless entertainment about women who were struggling, just like me. As much as these movies were fantasy, they still gave me hope that maybe, just maybe, there was somebody out there for me, and, just like the heroin in the movie, I would one day meet him.

So, we ended up seeing a silly movie starring Sandra Bullock that was forgotten almost as soon as I walked out the door of the theatre. But it provided me some much-needed happiness, even if it really didn't last.

Chapter Seventeen

RYAN

I committed myself to Alexis, in spite of my inner voice telling me this was the wrong thing to do. She was right, in a way – we both had suffered a devastating loss. The same devastating loss. So, we needed to lean on each other. Losing Mia was, by far, the worst tragedy of my life, but it somehow brought Alexis and me back together, against all the odds.

Of course, she dropped the assault charges against me, and told the prosecutor what had really happened. She even admitted to them that she had me arrested because she didn't want me to leave her.

I felt she was finally being honest with herself, so maybe, just maybe, she would start being totally honest with me as well.

We even attended a grief support group for parents who had lost a child. Alexis found the place, and told me that it would be good for the two of us to attend. It would help, she said, for us to hear other parents and their stories. We could see we weren't alone.

I was all for that, of course. I really wanted Alexis to get counseling, but she had refused that. So, when she said that she wanted us to attend this group, I thought that it was a step in the right direction.

And, to my surprise, Alexis also told me that she thought that it would be good for the two of us to get couples counseling with Dr. Halder. That really excited me, because she had always refused this step before.

"I think that it would help us," she said. "I really want this to work, and I know how much we've hurt each other throughout our lives together. Maybe Dr. Halder can help us stop tormenting each other."

I nodded. "Wow," I said. "Maybe you and I have a chance. Couples counseling can help us as a couple, and maybe you can also think about doing individual counseling. I know you have a lot of issues you need to work through."

"One step at a time," she said. "I'm not sure I'm ready for all that, but I would like to find a way for you and I to work through our issues in our relationship. I think that Dr. Halder can really help us with that."

I didn't press her, although I knew she desperately needed individual counseling. Mia was just the latest thing to happen to her, but, throughout her life, she'd struggled with a variety of issues that made her the way she was. It was her drug addiction, my father raping her, her parents disowning her. These issues were probably the tip of the iceberg. Combine that with the fact that she was born with brain chemicals that went haywire if she wasn't 100% diligent with her meds, and, sometimes, they still went haywire even if she was perfect with taking her meds. Such was the nature of bipolar disorder – meds work for a time and then they stop working.

She was a basket case, but she wasn't evil. I really believed there would come a time when she would be mentally healthy enough that we could make a real go of our relationship.

Despite what everyone who knew us told me.

Despite what my inner voice was screaming to me.

So, EVERY WEDNESDAY EVENING, we met our grief support group in a hospital that opened its cafeteria to us after hours. There typically were about 20 people who attended this group on a regular basis, and we were starting to get to know them and their stories. Most of the parents had lost a child through some type of disease, such as cancer, but there were a few whose child had died in an accident. And one whose child was murdered by her ex boyfriend.

The group leader first asked all of us how our week was going, and whether or not there was something special we wanted to share with the group. Then he structured the meeting with a topic for us to consider and encouraged us to relate our situation to the topic of the week. One week, for instance, we were to consider what we were grateful for. Another week we were asked to share with the group what coping strategies we were using, and how they were working.

For my part, I really tried to participate in this group. I spoke when it was my turn, and I tried to give advice when people were asking for it. I also attempted to give comfort to the people who appeared distraught and would cry because it was an anniversary or it was their child's birthday.

Unfortunately, Alexis didn't get as much out of the group. She was too obsessed with the fact that the one single woman there, who was the woman whose child was murdered, was apparently ogling me.

"I can't believe you didn't notice her and the way she was eyeing you," she said on the way home from the group one evening. It was after our fourth meeting, and this woman, whose name was Nicole, had come to the group in tears.

"My ex has a parole hearing," she told the group. "I can't believe it. He's only been in prison for two years. How can this be?"

None of us could believe it. True, the guy wasn't put away for first-degree murder, but, rather, manslaughter, as he had contended that he hadn't meant to kill the child. Rather, it was a shaken baby thing, where he shook the child so hard that he killed him. The prosecutor was successful in showing he never had the intent to kill, so the jury convicted him of manslaughter, not murder.

Still, a parole hearing after only two years?

Needless to say, Nicole was very upset that evening, and she and I met up in the hallway after both of us, coincidentally, had gone to the bathroom.

"Hey," I said, putting my hand on her shoulder. "It will be okay. They won't let that monster out of prison this soon."

At that, she started to bawl, so I put my arms around her and let her cry it out on my chest. She was wordless as her tears flowed freely. I stood there with my arms around her, trying to calm her down so both of us could go back into the room.

Alexis was soon out in the hallway, having come looking for me when I hadn't returned within fifteen minutes.

I knew, the second I saw Alexis's face as I stood there and held Nicole in my arms, that there was soon to be hell to pay. She narrowed her eyes at me, and scrunched up her face, turned on her heels, and went back into the room without a word.

Was I right about that.

I returned to the group about ten minutes later, and took my seat next to Alexis. Her body language was extremely cold, as she refused to look at me, and, when I reached for her hand, she abruptly snatched it away.

For the rest of the session, I sat there, uncomfortable, next to her. I spoke when it was my turn, and Alexis refused to speak, even though, usually, she did speak when it was her turn.

The topic that evening was forgiveness, and each of us were to say our thoughts about it. I told the group that I thought forgiveness was easy if you did one thing – tried to have empathy for the person who had wronged you. If you really tried to see where that person was coming from, then you might have some kind of sympathy for the person, no matter how shitty they were.

"Because, really, everybody has their own issues," I said. "If you can understand that, you can maybe come to some kind of terms with how they have treated you." It occurred to me that I was really addressing how I was feeling about Alexis, and I wondered if she was going to let me have it for basically calling her out in front of the group. Even if the group didn't necessarily know that was what I was doing.

In the car that evening, I was able to stop wondering. Because Alexis was furious, absolutely furious, about my hugging Nicole in the hall, and, yes, she also knew I was referring to her when I talked about forgiveness.

She was so angry about both things that she let me have it for both issues in one long tirade. The second we got to my car, she let loose with the accusations and the recriminations.

"What the hell happened in there?" she said to me as she buckled her seat belt.

I played dumb. "I don't know what you mean?"

"You. You apparently think you're just so perfect and I'm such a witch that you have to try to understand and take pity on me so you can forgive me. Yet, there you were, making out with another woman right there in the hallway. That's pretty goddamned rich of you, Ryan. News flash – you aren't the perfect golden boy you think you are. Tonight just proves that."

I sighed. "Alexis, Nicole was really distraught. I suppose you thought that I should have pushed her away from me, when she was absolutely falling apart about her child's murderer getting a parole hearing. You do know she's going to have to attend that hearing, don't you? I couldn't imagine anything worse than doing that."

"Oh, that's just so convenient for you, isn't it, Ryan? You're such a dumbshit. You walk around like you have no idea women are dripping for you wherever you go. You really don't see how that woman looks at you, do you? Do you?"

"Alexis," I began. "I'm not stupid. I know women are attracted to me. But what does that matter? I'm not a cheater, so they can eye me all they want. It's not in me to do something like that."

"Except with Nick," she said.

"That's different," I said. "You know he and I don't get into it except for when I'm not in a relationship with you. Besides, he and I haven't gotten into that for years. And you know this."

"Maybe so," she said. "But I know how you feel about him."

"How you feel about him, you mean," I said. "You're projecting. You have the hots for him and you always have. You think I can't see that, don't you?"

"Oh, no," she said. "You aren't going to do this to me. You aren't going to boomerang the conversation back to me and my failings. I won't let you do that."

"Okay, you're right," I said. "Let's talk about tonight. Now, Nicole was having a rough time, and I was trying to comfort her. But that really isn't the issue, is it, Alexis?"

"It's not?"

"No, it's not. The issue is that you don't trust me. And you never did. There has never been any indication that I've ever cheated on you, yet you've always accused me of it. I'm sorry, Alexis, that women find me attractive. I don't really know what to do about that, though. So, you have a choice here – either you learn to trust me, or you get out of this relationship. Because there's nothing I can do about the way I look. Sorry about that."

She crossed her arms. "I'm sorry, Ryan, but I don't believe you. I think you want to fuck that woman. I can see it in your eyes."

I sighed. "Really, Alexis? Really? What made you come to this conclusion?"

"I see the way you look at her," she said. "I don't want to come this group anymore." She paused for a few minutes. "I don't like the way you look at that woman, and I really don't like the shady way you make yourself look like such a great guy and make me look like a lunatic. Every one of those people around that table knew who you were talking about when you were talking about forgiveness."

"Alexis, don't you think that you're being slightly paranoid?" I said. "I was talking in general terms."

"General, my ass," she said. "Who else do you have to forgive in your life except for me? Your father, but I don't see you letting go of your anger about him anytime soon. That whole speech was directed right at me and I didn't like it one bit."

"Alexis, I'm sorry that you are paranoid about this, but, trust me, I wasn't thinking about you when I was talking about that. I was thinking about…" I stopped as I realized that Alexis was right. She *was* the only person in my life I had to forgive, except my father, and, as she said, I wasn't prepared to forgive him any time soon.

I finally conceded her point. "Okay, okay, I guess I was referencing you, but so what? I was trying to say I have empathy for you, because I know how much you struggle."

"Empathy or pity?" she said. "There's a fine line between those two concepts, Ryan. And I think you feel more pity for me than anything else."

I kept quiet as I silently regarded her words. They were biting, but they weren't far from the truth. I *was* with her out of pity, really. I hadn't even thought of it that way, but it was inescapable – I felt sorry for her and felt she needed me. And that was really a lot of the reason why the two of us were together at that moment.

I desperately tried to pivot away from this particular conversation, because to admit the truth to her would be devastating. "Empathy, not pity," I said. "I try to look through your eyes when I feel myself getting angry with you. It doesn't always work, but sometimes it does."

She raised an eyebrow. Somehow, she found a way to mash the two concepts together – that I pitied her and that she didn't trust me not to sleep with other women. "And

Nicole, she's really pity-worthy, isn't she? Since you're so obviously with me because you feel sorry for me, I can just imagine how much a woman like Nicole might get your juices going, Ryan. Well, why don't you just go to her, since I can see you're dying to. Make her the charity case that you so desperately need to make your pitiful life seem more worthwhile. Because I'm not going to do it anymore."

We had arrived at our house. I pulled into the driveway, shut off the car, and put my head on the steering wheel. "Fine," I said. "I'm tired of fighting, Alexis. I'm tired of fighting you and I'm tired of fighting for us. I had some hope when you said that you were willing to see Dr. Halder with me, but you've made 100 excuses for why you don't want to see him. So, I can only conclude that you really weren't serious when you proposed the two of us see him. And I seriously don't have the energy to go through this with you anymore, Alexis. I just don't."

I looked over at her and her face was no longer a mask of anger. She took a deep breath. "You're right, Ryan. I need to try to find a way to trust you. It's always been difficult for me to do that. I don't want us to break up, Ryan. I'm sorry for the things I just said to you."

I wondered if there was anything that would make our relationship work. Or if Nick was right – I was the walking definition of insanity. Doing the same thing, over and over, expecting a different result.

"Alexis, I'm serious. I can't do this anymore."

"Ryan, please. I'm sorry. I know I've resisted seeing Dr. Halder with you, and I don't really know why I have. I'm scared of what he's going to say to me, Ryan. I've always been afraid of shrinks."

I took a deep breath. There was something in me that still, even after everything that had happened between us, wasn't entirely ready to let go. I had no idea why. "One more chance," I said. "We go and see Dr. Halder on Tuesday after both of us get off of work or you're moving out of the house. I mean that."

"Okay," she said, beaming. "Thank you, Ryan. Thank you for giving me this chance. I'll go and see him with you. Hopefully, he can help us."

I tried to fight back my visions of Iris, which flashed in my brain as I sat there next to Alexis. "Yes, Alexis, maybe he can help us."

Even as I said the words, though, I knew that I was lying to myself.

Chapter Eighteen

The next day, after Alexis and I had our blow-out, I decided to make an appointment with Dr. Halder. I told Nick this when we met for our weekly beer.

"So," he said, as the two of us sat down. "How's the spawn of Satan doing?"

I smiled, in spite of myself. "Satan's spawn is doing about as well as she ever has. Which means she is continuing to torment me with jealous rages, when she's not accusing me of staying with her out of pity."

"Aren't you?" he said.

"Yes," I admitted. "At first, when she accused me of this, I tried to deny it. Then I thought about it and I realized my pity for her and her situation was really the only reason I'm still sticking around. So, we're going to see Dr. Halder together for some couples counseling. Hopefully, I can find another reason to stay with her. Because, right now, being with her is killing me."

Nick nodded his head. He was strangely sanguine about the news that Alexis and I were going for counseling. I expected that he would throw cold water on the entire idea, and tell me, again, how much of an idiot I was for staying with her.

"Go ahead," I said. "Tell me how much of a mistake I'm making."

He looked towards the entrance of the bar, and stood up when a drop-dead gorgeous woman came through the door. She was tall and thin and had large breasts. Her hair was thick and brunette, and her eyes were a gorgeous color of blue.

Nick raised his glass of beer as she nodded and headed over to our table.

"Ryan," he said. "I'm out of words to tell you how dumb you're being. I've decided another tactic."

As the woman headed to our table, I knew what this tactic was. "Hello, Nick," the woman said, kissing him on the cheek.

"Daniela," he said. "Good to see you. Daniela, this is Ryan. Ryan, Daniela."

Her face lit up as she extended her hand. "Good to meet you, Ryan," she said.

I sighed as I shook her hand. Not that I was angry with Nick for ambushing me. I knew his heart was in the right place. But I hated being ambushed all the same.

"And you, Daniela," I said to her.

"Well," Nick said. "I'm going to go and get us a round of drinks. You two pretend I'm not even here."

Daniela laughed. "I can see on your face that you weren't expecting to meet me. Leave it to Nick to lie to me like that."

Oh, man. "I'll be honest with you. Nick never said a word about this to me. And I'm terribly sorry, Daniela. I don't know what Nick told you, but my situation is terribly complicated right now. I'll be up front and tell you I'm not the guy you want to get involved with at the moment."

She looked disappointed, but she recovered nicely. "Oh, that's too bad. I think we could have gotten along really well."

I shook my head. "Maybe in another life. But, trust me, you don't want to hang around me. I'm going through a lot of crap right now." Then I chuckled lightly. "But don't let that deter you. Maybe you and I could be friends."

Even as I said that, though, I knew that Alexis would go absolutely ape-shit ballistic at the thought that I would ever have a "friend" who looked like Daniela.

"Maybe so," she said, putting her finely manicured hand on my arm. "Maybe so."

I looked over at Nick, who was deep in conversation with some woman over at the bar. I finally motioned him when he looked up, and he headed back over to the table with drinks in his hand. "A scotch for you, Ryan, and a dirty martini for you, Daniela. I remember you telling me how much you like these."

She politely took the martini and thanked Nick before announcing that she was going to powder her nose. She got up from the table and disappeared into the crowd.

"So," Nick said. "What do you think? If that woman can't take your mind off of Alexis, I don't know who will."

"Nick," I said. "I appreciate what you're trying to do. I really do. But I have to do things on my own terms and on my own schedule. You should know me well enough by now to understand that about me."

"I know," he said. "But I had to take a shot."

I sighed and shook my head. "The crazy thing is, Nick, I don't even know why I don't want to go out with Daniela. I mean, Alexis and I are trying this last-ditch thing with Dr.

Halder, but I don't have any hope that it's going to change anything at all between us. I guess I really…."

Nick looked at me expectantly. "Really, what, Ryan? Finish your thought."

I shook my head, embarrassed to admit that I still couldn't get that Iris woman out of my head. I had no idea why. She was creeping into my thoughts, more and more, especially since it appeared Alexis and I weren't going to be together too much longer.

"Nothing, nothing. I just don't feel like starting up anything new, Nick. I mean, my headspace is pretty screwed-up right now. I just lost a child. Alexis has been playing mind-fuck games. I just started my job and I'm trying to get acclimated over there. I don't know in what universe I would be good boyfriend material to somebody."

Nick shrugged. "You need something to take your mind off of Alexis," he said. "I love you, man, I really do. And to see you go through all of this bullshit…" He shook his head. "You deserve so much better than that. So much better."

I leaned a little closer to him. "Nick, do you ever think…"

He got my drift. "All the time, Ryan. But, you know, I'm committed to Rielle for now. Like you, though, I have no idea how long that will last. But, yes, Ryan, I do think about you and me together, and how much fun it was in the Hamptons." He smiled. "You know, Ryan, there are times when I feel like I could just give up women altogether and just settle down with a guy. I mean, why not? I swing both ways anyhow. And women are nothing but a pain in my ass 99% of the time."

I smiled. Sometimes I felt, in my heart of hearts, that I loved that guy more than I had ever loved anybody in my life. Most of the time, it was as a bro, but there were times when I started to question whether or not I truly was in love with him. After all, no woman had ever done anything for me other than stalk me, mind-fuck me, or both. Nick, on the other hand, had walked through fire with me. Every step of the way. He had been the only thing in my life that was healthy, with the possible exception of Sarah. Sarah always had my best interests at heart, too, but she lived on the Vineyard and I didn't see her as often as I would have liked.

Nick smiled. "And, yes, Ryan, if I ever decided to give up women, you would definitely be first on my list."

"I wasn't questioning that," I said. "Sometimes I miss you…and me…." I felt my face blushing crimson. "Oh, what am I talking about? I'm just kind of a low point in my life, and you, well, you've been the only person who has truly given a rat's ass about me. Except my sister."

Nick sat there quietly, drinking his beer. "I feel the same way about you," he said. "Rielle, well, you know how we get along. My kids are pure, though." He shrugged. "Maybe that's really all we can ask for in life. Have children and try not to screw them up too much. But your partner in life… well, let's just say it's not always an ideal situation. But, you get through the rough parts and hope you can see some light."

I knew what was coming next.

"And, you, Ryan, I'm sorry to say, have little chance of seeing light as long as you're with her. Sorry, though, I seriously don't think I'm really going to give up women. So, I don't think you and I are necessarily an option together. You need to get out there, Ryan, and find somebody that you can be with for real."

At that, Daniela was coming back to the table.

I took a deep breath. Maybe Nick was right.

Maybe I needed to give Daniela a chance.

So, for the rest of the evening, we all had drinks and I talked to Daniela. I found out that she was the CEO of a small Internet company that she had founded five years back and she lived near me in the Hallbrook area. She was smart, and funny, and breathtakingly gorgeous. She was probably the greatest woman on paper.

I made a mental note that, if Alexis and I didn't work out, maybe, just maybe, I would give Daniela a call.

But only after I went to find out more about Iris.

Chapter Nineteen

I took a deep breath as I headed back down to the Public Defender's Office. I had more of an idea on what I was going to say, as far as finding out where she was working. I was going to go with my last story about my being a process server she met in a bar. That seemed to go over okay the last time I was there at that office.

I felt a little bit guilty doing this, because Alexis and I were still going to try to work things out, but, at the same time, it wouldn't hurt to know how to find that woman. At least, that was what I told myself as I parked in a garage downtown, got my ticket, and headed to the white building that housed the PD's Office.

I went into the lobby and pushed the elevator button. Just then, two women came up and they also waited for the elevator.

"Did you go to Iris' wedding last weekend?" one of the women asked the other one.

"I did," she said. "How come you weren't there?"

"I had to work," she said. "I've got a murder trial coming up. How was it?"

My heart quickened as I listened to these women. Iris got married? Perhaps it was another Iris. Who also worked at the Public Defender's Office.

I shook my head. Iris was somewhat of an unusual name.

I guess I wasn't going to try to find this woman after all.

ALEXIS AND I went to see Dr. Halder that evening. I was very discouraged to find out that the woman that I couldn't stop thinking about was married. Not that this knowledge affected how I was feeling about Alexis. I still thought she and I were on the verge of completely breaking up.

I guess I really was looking forward to finding Iris. Now, well, I wasn't going to anymore. I had to put that woman out of my mind.

I got there directly after work, and Alexis came straight from her job as well. We hadn't really talked all that much since the blow-up in the car, so I found myself feeling strangely uncomfortable around her.

Alexis came in as I was sitting in the waiting room, reading a magazine and waiting for her. She sat down as well.

"I'm sorry I'm late," she said. "It's my first week back, and, well, they're really piling it up on me. I had three depositions to do today. Three. I really hate those, too."

"I wasn't worried," I said, although the way she was acting was strange. Almost like she was trying to cover something up.

I shook my head, and decided I was just going to have

to ignore my inner voice. There was absolutely no reason to throw shit back at Alexis, like she did to me.

"Good," she said, checking her watch. "Now, where is this Dr. Halder?"

I motioned to the closed door. "I think he has a crisis situation in there. I've been hearing a lot of crying and screaming coming out of there. Perhaps we need to just be patient."

Alexis, to my surprise, just nodded and said nothing about Dr. Halder seeing us late. I was prepared for her to really start going off about it, but she seemed pretty sanguine.

Ah, Alexis. There was just no telling how she would react to any given situation. I guessed it was a matter of who she was listening to – the angel on her shoulder or the devil.

"So," she said.

"So," I said.

She made a noise that showed she was mildly annoyed, but she didn't really talk to me. I didn't talk to her either. I was finding, more and more, that I simply had nothing really to say to her.

Finally, fifteen minutes later, Dr. Halder ushered out a crying woman. She brushed past us on her way to the receptionist, and I heard her making a follow-up appointment.

"Ryan," Dr. Halder greeted me. "Good to see you."

"You too," I said, standing up. Alexis remained seated. "Uh, Dr. Halder, this is my wife, Alexis."

Alexis finally got on her feet, and shook the doctor's hand. "Hello," she said. "It's good to meet you."

All of us went into his office and Alexis and I sat on the leather love seat.

"What brings the two of you here?" he asked, as a way to get us to start talking about what was going on.

I started. "Well, Dr. Halder, as you know, we recently lost a child," I said. "And…"

Alexis piped up. "I'm sure, Dr. Halder, that Ryan has told you all about me. I would imagine he's talked about how horrible I am for hours to you."

Dr. Halder started to scribble in his pad.

And we're off to a rousing start.

"Actually, Alexis," he said to her, "Ryan hasn't really focused so much on you lately." He looked at me and I nodded. I had given him free reign to tell Alexis whatever he needed to tell her, and I had signed waivers to this effect. "He has been distraught over losing Mia, and this has been what our sessions have mainly focused on."

Alexis looked like she didn't believe him about this. "Whatever," she said.

Dr. Halder shifted in his seat imperceptibly. "Alexis," he said to her. "Why did you decide to come with Ryan today?"

She drew a breath. "I love him. I love him so much. I don't think he realizes how much I love him. And I don't want to lose him. I can't lose him, but I know my behavior pushes him away. I need to learn how to treat him better."

Dr. Halder nodded. "I see. Now, tell me how you view your relationship with Ryan."

"Well," she began. "I have a lot of problems, and I seem to take them all out on him. And I have recently found out that he's staying with me out of pity. I can't stand that. We really don't communicate well, either."

Dr. Halder continued to write in his book.

We talked to Dr. Halder for two hours, with him scribbling in his notebook the entire time. Both of us told him our side of the story, and, by the end of it, he concluded we were suffering from severe co-dependency.

I got the gist of what he was saying to us. Co-dependency was one of those things that signified a relationship was toxic, because, really, there wasn't any purpose for our relationship except to enable both of our bad behaviors.

I couldn't disagree with him.

"So," Alexis said to him, "can you help us?"

"Of course," he said. "But you, Alexis, probably should look into individual counseling."

She didn't say anything, but I knew what she was thinking. She was considering the fact that maybe, perhaps, she would actually try to get some counseling. Not that I was so mentally healthy and together, but I was starting to feel I was, the more I got counseling on my own.

We finally got up and went to see about making another appointment. The receptionist scheduled us in for Wednesday of the following week, and the two of us went out the door.

"I'll see you when I get home?" I said to her.

"Uh, no," she said. "I'm going out with Rebecca tonight. We're going to see a movie."

I shrugged and went on home.

Chapter Twenty

Things between Alexis and I were strained after that counseling session, and she was becoming more and more distant. I felt alone.

So, I decided to get a dog. I didn't even consult Alexis about this, because I knew she would try to talk me out of it. She didn't like dogs. I, on the other hand, loved them. I felt that dogs, in general, bring so much to humans. And maybe I was seeking the love and companionship that I was craving during this time.

The love and companionship that I wasn't getting from my relationship with my wife.

It's better to ask forgiveness than permission I thought as I went to the local shelter. I had no idea what kind of dog I wanted. I thought that I would just know when I found the right one.

Kind of like I would just know when I found the right woman. Iris flashed through my mind and I willed that thought away. She wasn't available, but surely there was somebody out there who was right for me.

I got to the shelter and I looked around. There were little dogs and big ones, shy ones and gregarious ones. I bent down to look at the dogs who were in cages on the floor. I loved coming to the shelter, even if it disturbed me. I hated seeing the dogs confined like this, and I really hated knowing there were so many dogs who wouldn't get good homes.

"Can I help you?" a petite blonde girl, who looked to be in her early twenties, asked me.

"Yes," I said, pointing to two pit bull mixed dogs who were in a kennel together. There was something about these two that drew me in. "I'd like for you to take these dogs out so that I can pet them and walk them."

At that, she got the two dogs out. They were energetic and extremely excited to be getting out of their kennel. The blonde girl, who explained her name was Kelly, put the two dogs on a leash and I took them out into the yard to walk them.

I walked with the dogs a short distance and then sat down on the grass, underneath a tree. The dogs sat down next to me, their tongues hanging out in the heat. I pet them, and they licked my face. "So, what do you guys think?" I asked. "How would you like to come home with me and keep me company while my wife virtually ignores me? What do you think about that?"

One of the dogs, whose name was Fric, wagged his tail when I said that, as if he understood.

"Yeah, you would love that," I said. "You guys will be so spoiled, I can guarantee you that. Nothing but the best. Well, sorry, I can't give you sirloin steak every night, but you'll get the best dog food, lots of bones, lots of exercise and lots of love, of course. That goes without saying."

The other dog, Frac, also started to wag his tail, and he

rolled on his back on the grass. At that, Fric got into the act, jumping on top of Frac. The two of them wrestled in the grass, growling and snapping playfully. Then Fric took off, Frac running after him. The two of them ran around the grounds, leaping and bounding over one another.

I imagined these two puppies at my home, running around my backyard, and I knew.

I knew these two were about to become two of the most spoiled dogs in the world.

I put the leash back on them, and I went inside.

"Hello," I said. "These are the dogs I want. But is it okay if I change their names?"

"Certainly," Kelly said. "They're new here, and they were strays, so we really don't know what their actual names are, anyhow."

I smiled. "Brutus and Maximus," I said, thinking of Sarah's dog, Coriolanus. I always loved that name, Coriolanus, and thought Roman names were appropriate for noble dogs like these two were.

I went through the adoption paperwork, which took about an hour, and then retrieved my two pups.

I loaded them into the Escalade, and secured them in the dog kennel I bought for this occasion. They willingly got into the kennel. It was if they knew they were going to a better place than where they were staying. They seemed excited to be going with me.

I felt the same way about them.

Perhaps these two beautiful creatures would help cure my loneliness. Maybe they couldn't. But, come what may, they were mine and I was theirs.

And I couldn't be happier about that.

UNFORTUNATELY, ALEXIS WASN'T AS THRILLED. She came home from work and saw the two dogs out in the backyard. "What are those two mutts doing here?" she asked, crossing her arms on her chest.

"These are my two dogs," I said.

Alexis picked up on the fact that I referred to the dogs as "mine," not "ours," and she was none too happy about it. "Your dogs, Ryan?" she said. "Your dogs? Are you the only person in this house now?"

I drew a breath. I knew she was going to react like this. I also knew, in my heart, that I referred to the dogs as "mine" because I didn't think that Alexis would be around much longer. "Yes, they're mine. I got them at the shelter. Their names are Brutus and Maximus."

"Take them back."

"I will not."

"You didn't consult me." Her hands were on her hips and her face was a mask of rage. "How can you just get two mutts without even asking me?"

"Alexis, I…" I didn't finish that sentence, because it would only cause a huge fight.

"You what?"

"Nothing. I just need companionship, that's all. If you won't give that to me, maybe these two puppies will."

"Oh, that's bullshit. Maybe if you want me to give you 'companionship' you might think about treating me a little bit better. Did you ever think of that?"

I sighed. "I'm not taking them back. They're here to stay. Like it or leave."

At that, she stormed off, went into our bedroom and slammed the door.

I went into the yard and threw the ball around with the

dogs for the next hour. And I felt more happiness during that hour than I had felt in a long, long time.

Chapter Twenty-One

I finally just decided that, in addition to our counseling, I would try one last-ditch effort to bring Alexis and me closer together. I decided that maybe Alexis and I just needed to get away. Change our scenery. Maybe it was time to get to Italy. I could visit my winery, and we could just relax. See if we could reconnect.

It was certainly worth a shot, as long as Alexis actually did go through with her intention to get individual counseling. She had, thus far, seemed to be doing better as far as not using, so that was a plus. She still seemed depressed and she often isolated herself when she was home, but she seemed to be trying to get better.

So, I made a decision to surprise her. I called a limousine, and I made a decision to blindfold her and take her to my private plane. Then we would go off to Italy, and, hopefully, we could have a good time. Maybe this trip would take our minds off what happened with Mia.

I got the limousine and the blindfold, and I had some champagne chilling in the mini-bar in the car. And then I headed back to our house. I knew Alexis would probably be home, as it was late, so she should probably be back from work.

I got to our house, and turned the key. Alexis didn't seem to be around anywhere. I looked around the house, and wondered if she was upstairs in our room. Lately, she made the effort to not lock herself in our room. She at least tried to come out and have dinner with me in the evening. Sometimes we even watched a movie together.

She was trying.

I walked upstairs and then stopped. I heard Alexis giggling in our room behind the door. I stood there, trying to ascertain if she was on the phone with somebody.

She wasn't. I also heard the unmistakable voice of Paul.

My heart quickened as I heard Alexis groaning, and Paul's voice.

"Give it to me," Paul said. "God, you're skin is so soft."

I actually felt conflicted about this. On the one hand, I was angry. But, more than anger, I felt relief. Relief because I finally had my answer on whether or not I was going to stay with Alexis.

I decided, however, to make a stand. Humiliate them both.

I opened the door.

"Hello, Alexis," I said, as both of them jumped. "And, hello, Paul. I guess I don't need to tell you that you're fired."

Alexis shook her head rapidly. "Ryan, I can explain," she said.

I thought to myself *explain. How can you possibly explain something like this?* "I'm sure you can, Alexis. Maybe this is all an accident. You accidentally got naked and Paul accidentally put his cock inside of you. Well, okay, then. Since this is obviously an accident, perhaps I should just look the other way."

I stood there and neither of them looked like they knew what to do. I guess they wanted me to discreetly turn around and walk out so they could get their clothes on.

I wasn't going to give them that kind of respect. I wanted both of them to twist in the wind. So I stood there with my arms crossed in front of me.

Paul finally decided that I wasn't going to let him discreetly sneak out of the bed, so he hung his head, and, with a sheet around him, he slinked into the bathroom. Needless to say, he didn't meet my eyes.

"Okay, Alexis," I said. "Please follow Paul out the door. And never come back. I'll pack up your things and put them into storage."

Alexis started to look panicky. "Ryan, please, I'm so sorry about this. I just have been so lonely and desperate these days, and you've been so far away emotionally. Please, though, Ryan, please don't leave me over this. I'll get help. I'll go into sex addiction therapy if you need me to. I'll do whatever you need for me do, Ryan. And this wasn't love. It was just sex. I love you."

I sighed. "Alexis, I know we haven't had sex since we've been married. So perhaps this is at least partially my fault that you ended up in bed with Paul. But that doesn't matter. Your fault, my fault, both of our fault, whatever. It's over, Alexis. It's over, and, quite frankly, I couldn't be happier about that. As I said the other night, I'm tired of fighting for us."

Just like that, I was done. For real.

But Alexis wasn't about to go down without a fight. "Ryan, please don't. We just started counseling together. Let's keep going to counseling, and I promise I'll start individual counseling, and I'll do whatever you want. Please, Ryan."

"No, Alexis," I said, feeling strangely calm. "No. Just stop. Stop, Alexis. It's over. Finito. And, I'm sorry, but I couldn't feel happier about this."

"Ryan, no." Alexis was shaking her head. She got out of the bed, finally, completely naked. She took my face in her hands, and tried to kiss me. "I want you to make love to me, Ryan. I want you to. But you don't. You don't. Please, Ryan, make love to me. I don't want Paul."

I sighed. "Alexis, as I said, I know we haven't had sex since we've been married. But don't you see? Don't you see that's part of the problem? I haven't wanted to be intimate with you, Alexis. I haven't wanted to. So you go to Paul. Okay. I don't blame you. But none of that changes the fact that you and I are, at long last, done."

Alexis was finally beginning to get it. That I was really, and truly, done with her. So, predictably, she went the other way. She got really angry.

"Ryan," she said. "You can't divorce me. If you do, then you'll see what happens. I'll air all of your dirty laundry out for everyone to see. I'll go to your work, and I'll even go to the media. I'll tell them just what a sicko your dad is."

"Alexis, is that all you got? Really? My father was severely abusive to me, but so what?" Even as I said that, though, I knew there was more. Also, I couldn't forget that my father was a rapist. I knew that about him. I knew what he did to Alexis. It just occurred to me that what my father did to her was a large reason why I stayed with Alexis even though it was always clear to me that she and I were poison together. I felt guilty about him doing that to her.

"Yes he was abusive to you. He's a sick, sick man, Ryan. And he's a prominent man in this city, even now. He might not still be a CEO, but he's a billionaire, and a major phil-anthropist. Perhaps the media needs to know exactly what kind of a man he is."

I hesitated, but only briefly. "Do what you need to do, Alexis," I said. "I have no love for that man anymore. I don't really care what happens to him, to be absolutely honest with you. It won't work to blackmail me."

Alexis opened her mouth, and I put my hand up. "Alexis, please, just don't speak anymore. There's absolutely nothing that you can say to me that will make an iota of difference. Not one iota of difference. So, please, just leave this house, and take Paul with you."

It was then that I realized that Paul had not yet emerged from the bathroom. I went in there, and he was sitting there, on the john, fully clothed, his head in his hands.

"Paul," I said to him. "You need to leave with Alexis."

"Ryan, I'm so sorry," he said. "I don't even have an excuse for this."

"You don't need one," I said. "I'm really not angry. You've done me a favor, really. But you're still fired."

I thought he really had an excuse, though. Alexis was a beautiful woman who could be very persuasive. Not many men would be able to resist that.

Paul exited the bathroom, not looking at me at all. "Come on, Alexis," he said to her. "Let's get out of here before things start to get ugly."

"I'm not leaving. And you, Ryan, can't make me."

"Alexis, really," I said. "Seriously, you need to leave. You need to get out of here before I call the police and have you kicked out for real." I thought about how that would be sweet, sweet irony – calling the cops on her, just like she did me all those months ago.

"You can't have me kicked out of my own home," she said.

I let out my breath. "Okay. Well, if you will excuse me."

At that, I went to the other room to call Sheldon.

"Hello, Ryan," Sheldon said when he answered the phone. "What can I do for you?"

"You need to file for divorce for me tomorrow," I said. "First thing. And get all those restraining orders that come with filing first, could you?" I knew Kansas divorce law. Sheldon had counseled me on it several times, and I knew the first person who filed would be the one who would be able to kick out the other person and get a restraining order against them.

"On it," he said. "I already have the papers drawn up."

And he did. He had them on file since Alexis and I got married. He and I both knew this day was coming and we really needed to hit the ground running.

"Thanks."

"So, what was the final straw?" he asked.

"I'll tell you later. But you can put the word 'infidelity' on your petition and it wouldn't be a lie. Not even Alexis can deny that at this point."

"I see. You really don't have to tell me any more."

"Okay," I said. "Tomorrow. File the papers and get the restraining order. Thanks."

I went back into the bedroom. Paul was gone, and Alexis was sitting on the bed. "Ryan, let's talk. Please, sit down, and let's talk."

"No," I said. "I'm going to bed." And then I went into the guest room, which was where I slept, more often than not, and plopped down on the bed.

Tomorrow the papers would be filed and, by the end of the day, there would be a restraining order against Alexis.

Ryan Gallagher

And I finally, at long last, would be free.

Chapter Twenty-Two

The next day, just as Sheldon promised, he filed my petition for divorce and obtained a restraining order against Alexis. That was the first step to getting her out of the house.

The second step, of course, was deciding where it was that she was going to go. I couldn't just kick her out without any means. She would absolutely crack if I did that. She was right on the edge, anyhow, and I really didn't want to be responsible for her possibly spiraling into such a pit that she could never emerge. Or worse.

She wasn't my problem anymore. I couldn't continue to make her my problem anymore, because I had to be happy. Yet, I couldn't just let her go into the night with no place to go.

I started calling her friends, one by one. I went down the line, and all of them told me the same thing – they loved Alexis, but they couldn't take her. Not that I blamed them – Alexis was a handful for sure.

I finally found somebody who was willing to take her in

– Rebecca, who was one of Alexis' oldest friends. "Sure, Ryan, I would be happy to," she told me. "And I know about keeping her med compliant, because my sister's a nurse, and I've learned a lot from her. What do you need for me to do?"

"Please come to my house this evening at 6. I have a restraining order against her, and it's going to get ugly. I'm going to have to kick her out, probably with a police escort. If you could just be there to make sure that she comes home with you, that would mean the world to me. And to her as well."

"I'll be there."

I was relieved. I didn't hate Alexis. I loved her, but not in the way that she always wanted me to. I couldn't be with her anymore, but I also felt responsible for making sure she could land on her feet. Rebecca would go a long way to making sure that this happened.

I WENT HOME THAT EVENING, and waited for Rebecca to show up so that I could present Alexis with the restraining order. She did show, right at 6, so it was time for me to make my move.

Alexis had prepared a four-course dinner, and there were candles burning on the table when I got home. "Ryan," she said. "I'm so happy you're home. Look, I made your favorite meal." Then she looked at Rebecca. "Hello, Rebecca. I'm so sorry, I didn't realize that you were coming. Otherwise, I would have made extra."

"Oh, that's okay, Alexis," she said.

Alexis looked confused. She looked at both of us, her

hands on her hips. I felt bad that she didn't know what was about to happen, but it couldn't be helped.

I smelled *coq au vin* wafting through the dining room.

I seriously doubted that she made this food. She couldn't cook. I was quite sure that she had somebody come in and cook.

"This isn't going to work," I said. "You don't live here anymore. Rebecca is here to make sure you have a place to stay from now on, or at least until you can land on your feet. And you will land on your feet, Alexis."

"What do you mean?" she asked me. "Of course I live here. I'm your wife."

At that, I handed her the order that the judge had signed. The order that said that she could no longer be on the premises.

She read it, and her face got white. "What the hell is this?"

"What do you think it is? It's an order telling you to get out."

"When did you get this?"

"This morning." I drew a breath. "I filed for divorce and a restraining order at the same time. You need to leave, Alexis. You don't live here anymore."

"I won't leave," she said.

"Okay, then, I'll just have to make you leave." I looked over at Rebecca, who nodded her head, and then I picked up my phone and called the police.

As I started to talk, Alexis grabbed the phone out of my hand. "Please don't do this, Ryan. I have no place to go."

"That's why Rebecca is here."

At that, Rebecca put her arm around Alexis, but Alexis wasn't having it. She forcefully took Rebecca's arm from around her shoulder and glared at her. "I'm not going with you, Rebecca."

"Alexis, you have to come with me," Rebecca said. "You can't stay here. Ryan told me that you're not welcome here in this house anymore. You can stay with me until you can find a place of your own. And I'll make sure that you stay med compliant."

"You can't do this to me, Ryan," Alexis said, ignoring Rebecca. "I'll die without you. I hope you know that."

I took a deep breath, remembering what Dr. Halder said to me about co-dependency. Alexis was dependent upon me, because I guess that I made it that way for my own reasons. She was also extremely manipulative. She was attempting to do what she always did – guilt me into keeping her in the house and with me. I had to be strong and do what I had to do, come what may. Of course, I knew that she was right, too – she probably *would* go off the deep end without support.

That couldn't be my concern. My only concern had to be for myself and my own happiness. I couldn't help it if she had made her bed by alienating the people closest to her, especially me. If I let her get away with this, then she would keep on doing it, and then try to emotionally black-mail me into letting her stay.

"Alexis, I'm sorry. You're going to have to go and stay with Rebecca and then find a place of your own. You can't live here anymore with me."

Now she was pacing around the floor. "You can't do this. I can't handle this. I just can't handle this. I lost Mia, and if I lose you too, I will literally die. You want that on your head, Ryan? Do you?"

I crossed my arms. "Alexis, of course I don't want that on my head. But I have no choice in the matter. You finally crossed the line. And you were so stupid about it, too. Fucking him in our bed at a time when you knew I would be coming home. I really don't understand why you would do that unless you wanted to get caught. So, if you wanted to get caught, then I suggest you take the consequences of getting caught."

"I'm not leaving."

"You *are* leaving. And if I need to get the cops involved, I will." I was determined that *she* was going to be one who was going to leave, not me. It was my house, and I shouldn't have to be the one who would have to stay in a depressing hotel room. "Now, if you will excuse me, I need to make a phone call."

Alexis grabbed a kitchen knife and brandished it. "Put that phone away, Ryan, right now."

I rolled my eyes and made a split decision to call her bluff. That might be a bad idea, because Alexis was desperate and capable of anything, but I knew in my heart that she wouldn't use that knife. So, I kept dialing the phone, and Alexis lunged at me. The knife got dangerously close to my naval.

For her part, Rebecca was standing in the corner, her hand covering her mouth. She looked scared. I felt for her, and I hoped that she wasn't going to change her mind about taking Alexis in.

The police dispatcher answered the phone. I had decided not to call 911, as this wasn't really a true emergency. "Leawood Police Department, how may I assist you?" the dispatcher said to me.

"Yes, this is Ryan Gallagher," I began and then gave my address. "I have a restraining order against my wife and she refuses to leave."

"Yes sir, we'll have an officer over shortly."

I hung up the phone and looked at Alexis, who was still holding the knife close to my body. I calmly took the knife out of her hand, and she collapsed on the floor in tears. She hugged her body and rocked back and forth while she sobbed loudly.

In spite of all that had happened, and everything she did, it gave me no great joy to see her like this. I knew she was in pain. I also knew she might end up in the hospital again. Or worse.

But I also knew I had to be firm. Whatever happened to her after she left this house wasn't my problem anymore.

The police arrived in about twenty minutes, and I invited them in. By then, Alexis was a complete and total basket case. She was sitting on the floor and whimpering while shaking her head rapidly back and forth.

A female officer went over to her while I showed the other officer the paperwork I had that showed that Alexis was no longer welcome in this house. "Miss, you're going to have to come with me," she said.

I talked to the male officer. "Can you make sure she leaves with Rebecca?" I said, pointing to the poor girl who was going to be saddled with Hurricane Alexis. But she looked like she wasn't going to change her mind about taking Alexis in, so I was grateful for that.

"We will make sure she leaves with her friend. If she comes back here, she will be arrested. You just have to call us."

Alexis was on her feet, still sobbing, and the female officer had her arm around her and was gently ushering her out the door. I could hear the officer explaining to Alexis what would happen if she came back into the house, which was that she would be arrested, and I saw Alexis shaking her head. I doubted she understood what the officer was saying in that moment. She didn't seem to be comprehending much.

Rebecca was following closely behind Alexis and the police officers. She gave one last look at me and nodded. I nodded back to her and mouthed the words "thank you." At that, she nodded to me again.

"Thank you for coming," I said to the male officer, whose badge indicated that his last name was Miller.

"Not a problem," he said. "If your wife attempts to come back into the house, just give me us a call, and we'll be back."

I nodded and showed him out the door.

As I shut the door, I knew this was only the beginning. But that didn't matter. Alexis was gone, and, for now, that was all that really mattered.

Chapter Twenty-Three

After Alexis left I just felt relieved. Absolutely, completely relieved. In the back of my mind, I knew the hell was only beginning, but it would at least be a fresh hell. It would at least be a change.

I went into my bedroom and just lay down on the bed and listened to the silence. There was nobody else in the house, and this was a feeling that I hadn't had before. I tried to drink in the emptiness, tried to feel it. As soon as I did, I realized that I had mixed emotions about it all. The profound relief gave way to a feeling of loneliness. Isolation. I was truly alone, perhaps for the first time in my entire life, and I didn't really know how to feel about it.

But that was okay. It was truly okay that I was alone. It was better to be alone than to be with somebody who was absolute poison for me.

Besides, I had Brutus and Maximus to keep me company, and they truly did. They were beautiful, well-behaved dogs, and they were getting more and more that way, as I was taking them to puppy training classes every week.

But I was alone, as far as human companionship went, and, as I fully realized that, something happened. I thought about Mia and really allowed myself to feel her loss. All this time, I had pushed my feelings down because I had to. I had to be strong for Alexis, and I also had to deal with the crisis our relationship had become. There was so much going on that I really wasn't feeling my absolute devastation over losing my daughter.

I finally did in that moment after Alexis left, and I cried for the first time since I saw her crib empty. I let my tears flow for the rest of the evening as I went into her room and sat down on the rocking chair. I picked up one of her stuffed animals and stared at her crib and I just let loose the tears.

Eventually, I crawled into my empty bed and hugged the pillow and fell into a deep sleep.

THE NEXT DAY, I GOT THE CALL FROM SHELDON. Alexis had contacted her attorney, and they were ready to go to war.

"I figured that," I said, feeling relieved that Alexis apparently didn't fall apart when she left the house. "How are they going to get around the terms of the prenup?"

"They can't. They're just blowing smoke. I'll email you what they're demanding. It's pretty laughable, really."

I went to my email and downloaded the attachment, which was a correspondence from her attorney. Sheldon was right – it *was* laughable. They were demanding $50 million in cash, the de Kooning painting and maintenance in the amount of $50,000 a month.

In spite of myself, I burst out laughing. I had been

married to her for less than six months, yet she was essentially demanding a little less than half of everything I owned.

I called Sheldon back. "Tell her lawyer okay, and I'll throw in my Cezanne while I'm at it."

He chuckled back. "I admit, that's a ballsy opening salvo. But, don't worry, the prenup is the prenup. Alexis will get her $10 million that she signed for, and that will be that. I really don't know how she plans to get out of that, as she wasn't under duress, she had time to consider the details and she had her attorney look at it before she signed it."

"Well, I can imagine. She'll probably claim that she wasn't in her right mind when she signed it. And for Alexis, that's not far wrong. She usually isn't in her right mind."

"As long as she was lucid and could understand the document, then her mood disorder cannot be used to state that she wasn't in her sound mind when she signed the prenup."

"But I have no doubt that she'll try."

"Well, I just wanted to give you a call about that. Oh, and there's a hearing already set about the temporary restraining order. It's tomorrow at 1:30."

"That's good. Maybe we can make it permanent?"

"Probably not. The most we can hope for is to extend the restraining order until the divorce is final. Then, after the divorce is final, the restraining order will become final."

"Good enough," I said.

Then I went to work, calling Nick from my car.

"Hey," he said. "What's going on?"

"Let's meet tonight for dinner, huh? I got news."

NICK AND I MET FOR DRINKS AND DINNER that evening, and I told him what happened.

He laughed. "I can't believe you finally did it. Good for you." We clinked our glasses together after he said that. "That was a long time coming. A long time coming."

"I know. But, Nick, it's weird. I mean, I'm happy I finally did it. But, at the same time, I feel almost empty. We've been together, on and off, since we were 13 years old. She's really been my only real relationship in my adult life, as sad as that sounds."

"That is sad, really," Nick said. "That's sad that you've wasted so much time on her."

"It's sad that I've wasted so much time, period. On so many things. My drug addiction, Alexis, all of that. What I wouldn't give to have all those years back. All those years where I was an absolute waste."

"You can't live with regrets. They do you no good, buddy. Unless you learn from them and you vow never to repeat them. Which I assume you're doing."

"I am. But I have to admit that I feel just a little bit lost. Unmoored." I shook my head. "I have to figure out what my next step is in life, and, I admit, it's not necessarily going to be easy."

"It never is. But I have faith in you, buddy. You'll figure it all out soon enough."

I nodded my head and sipped my beer.

"Hey," he said. "Don't look like that. This is a good thing."

"I know. But, even so, it's going to take some adjusting."

"Goes without saying. In the meantime, Daniela is dying to have a date with you. I suggest you give her a call. It's about time that you get out there and live a little."

I took a deep breath. Nick was right – it was time to get

back out there. That Iris woman seemed to not be on the market anymore, so there wasn't a point in seeing about her. And it was about time that I found somebody who made me happy.

"Okay. I guess I can take Daniela out. I mean, it wouldn't hurt, would it?"

"Nope. It wouldn't hurt at all."

"Thanks, man. You're golden."

He smiled and took a sip of his beer. "Hey. Would you like to come over this weekend? Rielle and the girls are visiting her mother."

I knew what he was getting at, and I was sorely tempted. Being with Nick, sometimes, was exactly what I needed. And this happened to be one of those times.

"Yeah, sure. I'll bring the beer."

He smiled and took another sip of his scotch. He raised his glass. "To you and your new single life. You're gonna love it."

"I know I will," I said.

And I knew that he was right.

It was just going to take awhile.

Chapter Twenty-Four

The months went by, and I got more into work and handling my divorce. It was getting easier and easier to do, and Sheldon was an excellent divorce lawyer, so there was never a question on whether or not I would prevail. I knew that I would.

Not that Alexis didn't try. She did. She dragged me into countless depositions where all kinds of dirty laundry was brought out into the open. Things that I never wanted to think about. They were also irrelevant, and Sheldon howled every time the lawyer started to ask me about my drug use or my crazy mother or abusive father. He objected to all of these questions, but I still had to answer them. The objections were only for the record.

I had to dredge it up, but I didn't really mind. It was all cathartic. And I was finding that anything that was cathartic was something that was helpful to me. Because I really needed that – I needed a way to get my feelings and emotions about my life into the open, and fighting with

Alexis for total control of all my property was one way of doing just that.

Finally, Sheldon had enough. He called Alexis' lawyer when he wanted to drag us into yet another deposition and read him the riot act. "I'm going for a protective order that states that my client is not going to have to answer any other questions. If you send a subpoena for him to attend this latest deposition, I'm going to quash it and have you charged with abuse of process. You're right on the edge, there, pal, and you know it."

Sheldon and the other guy went back and forth several more times, and, finally, Sheldon got off the phone and told me that I wasn't going to have to attend anymore depositions. "And I'm going to file a motion with the judge to make sure that you don't have to do anymore of these damn things. It's pretty clear that Alexis is abusing the judicial process to try to get back at you."

I was non-plussed about it. I didn't really care anymore. Alexis could do what she wanted to. She was out of the house, having lost her bid to come back in, of course, and that was all that mattered to me.

Eventually, we were divorced. Alexis got her $10 million, and I also threw in a Porsche for her. I figured it was the least I could do at that point. I didn't hate her. I still pitied her. But I knew that, at long last, we were totally done. And that was something that was completely fine with me.

We met at the courthouse to get our divorce finalized. That was the first time that I had seen her in several months – since the last deposition. She looked heartbroken, and, for just a second, my heart went out to her. She wasn't a bad person. She was just severely messed up.

"Hi, Ryan," she said. "I guess this is it, huh?"

"Yes, I guess it is."

"It doesn't seem real. I mean, you've been there throughout my whole life, it seems. There hasn't been a period of time in my life when I thought that you and I were really through. Even during the times that we have broken up before, I always thought that you and I would be together in the end. Always."

I didn't feel the same, but I didn't tell her that. That would just be rubbing salt into the wound. "Well, Alexis, I know what you're saying. It is weird knowing that you and I are finally over. But that's how it has to be. We've hurt one another enough for several lifetimes. At some point, you have to simply admit defeat. And that's what I'm doing right now. Admitting defeat. You win, Alexis. You win by default, because I refuse to play anymore."

She took a deep breath. "I'm sorry, Ryan. I'm sorry for cheating on you, and I'm sorry for all the crap I put you through. And I'm really sorry that I finally pushed you away for good. I don't even know why I did that. You were right, though – I did want to get caught in bed with Paul. There was a very big part of me that doesn't feel worthy of you, I guess. At least that's what my therapist says."

"Your therapist?" I wondered when that started. "Good for you, finally seeing somebody. You really need that, you know."

"I know." She hung her head. "I hope you don't hate me, Ryan. I love you. I hope you know that. I'll always love you."

I didn't tell her those words back to her. I wasn't feeling them, so I didn't say them. "You'll be fine, Alexis. You're going to land on your own two feet without me."

I took the stand in front of the judge and I answered all

of Sheldon's questions. The judge signed off on the judgment that was prepared for him – the judgment that decreed that Alexis and I were divorced.

And, just like that, I was free for good.

Chapter Twenty-Five

After the divorce was final, I resumed my physical relationship with Nick. It wasn't a regular thing, just an occasional one, but it was something that did make me feel better about myself and my situation. He had a way of bringing me out of my dark times. He always had that ability. I guess the reason why he had this ability was because he was the only thing that was ever constant in my life. He had never lied to me. Never screwed me over. Always, always, always had my back.

He was the person who got me through my dark periods in one piece. I literally owed my life to him. He never gave up on me, even when I really wanted to give up on myself.

And he and Rielle were going through a rough period in their marriage. Nick wasn't one to stray if he was happy. There was a period of time with Rielle when he was happy, and he didn't stray. But he was increasingly becoming more and more unhappy with her, and it showed.

We would get together on occasion after we had our

drinks at the bar or dinner or whatever, and would go to my house. In the dark, we would suck each other off and then watch a movie. These evenings were probably the few times when I felt comfortable and not so alone.

I sensed he was feeling the same way. He confided in me that he was feeling as isolated as I was, even though he was still married and was living under the same roof as his wife.

"Yeah, it sucks," he said after one of our encounters. "I hate living this way."

I had the feeling that he got as much out of our oral encounters as I did.

As FOR THE DATING SCENE – it was okay. I was taking Daniela out, but there were other women that I was seeing as well. I was sleeping with all of them.

There was Erica, who was 28 and worked as a publicist. A willowy brunette with incredible legs and a wicked sense of humor, Erica and I had some good times in bed and out.

Then there was Brigitte, who was a cellist with the Kansas City Symphony. She was Dutch, gorgeous, spoke five languages, and was wildly talented on the cello. Her talents extended to other areas as well, I was increasingly finding out.

I had no desire to get serious with any of them. Not Daniela, not Brigitte, and not Erica. Not that there was anything wrong with them, of course, because there wasn't. On the contrary, they were all gorgeous, intelligent, and accomplished.

I was just having fun, though, perhaps for the first time in my life. Not that there was never a period of time when I was a player – I certainly was in my college years whenever

Alexis and I were broken up. But I was so wasted all those years – I was high all the time, so I really couldn't appreciate these women like I should have.

Now I wasn't on drugs anymore, so taking out these women was just fun for me. Nothing more than fun.

Unfortunately, as how it often happened, these women increasingly hinted around that they were much more serious about me than I was about them. Such as the evening that Brigitte casually mentioned that she was going home to visit her parents in Amsterdam during her break from the Symphony, and she would love for me to go.

"My parents live in a gorgeous chateau by the Amstel River. I told them all about you, and they would love to meet you," she said over dinner one evening at my house.

I smiled. I had traveled to Amsterdam when I lived in Europe, and I loved it. I tended to really gravitate towards the old European cities, anyhow, because I was fascinated by the architecture and the history of these places. And, I had to admit that, during this period of time, the seedier parts of this particular city really drew me in as well.

"When are you going to visit them?" I asked her, thinking that it would be nice to get out of the country. That was really the only reason why I was considering her invitation – I wanted to get out of the country.

"In six months," she said hopefully, while she dished out salad onto both of our plates.

I opened my mouth, and then shut it again. Six months? I could be anywhere in six months. "We'll see," I said. "Here, have some more garlic bread and wine."

Daniela and Erica said similar things. They talked about traveling with me as well. Daniela mentioned that she often vacationed in Switzerland, and was an expert skier. I was, as well, having mastered the black diamond years before. She was going back in December, and she pictured us on the slopes together.

I put her off, though, like I did Brigitte.

And Erica, as well, who said that she was going to be traveling to New Zealand on business in a few months, and would I like to come along?

I had the exact same answer. "We'll see," I said, without elaborating on that.

"I hope that you can make it, Ryan," Erica said to me. "I don't know if you've ever been down there, but that country is probably one of the most beautiful places on earth."

I knew that it was. I had gone there on a backpacking trip when I was on winter break one year at Harvard. Of course, it was summer down there in December, and I thought that this trip was among the best I had ever taken.

But I couldn't commit to going with Erica, so I just said "I don't think I can get off of work. Maybe next time, though, huh?"

I felt badly about stringing these women along. They were amazing women – beautiful, smart, cultured, funny, and kind. I should have been jumping at the chance for a serious relationship with any one of them, but I wasn't.

I knew that I was healing, slowly healing, from all that had happened to me, and my dating these women helped that along. I felt selfish, like I was using these women for my own purpose. I didn't really want to face up to an empty home, and I really did enjoy their company. I didn't see a future with any of them, and, of course, I didn't tell them that at all. But I still felt better when I was with them.

Yet I still felt lost and alone. But it was still one helluva lot better than being slowly poisoned by Alexis. I was still grieving Mia, of course, but I did it in my own time and in my own way.

Then something happened that changed my entire life and rocked my entire world.

Chapter Twenty-Six

I decided to go out with a bunch of people from work one Friday evening. We were going to Harry's Bar, an upscale cigar bar in the Westport District of the city. Westport was the place where many bars were located, and I liked this one in particular. It was trendy, but not overly so. And this bar had a decidedly mature clientele, in that there were very few drunken 21-year-olds who came to this place. Most people in there were 25 and up. The drinks were strong and the food was decent.

We were all sitting around in a group around the table. I was thinking about calling Daniela or one of the other women I was seeing and asking her to meet up with us. But, for the time being, I was just having fun hanging out with the people who worked with me.

Thank God I decided not to call one of my girlfriends, because my breath caught when I saw *her*. Iris. She was sitting alone at a table. She looked like she was waiting for somebody, because she kept looking over at the door. I saw her checking her watch several times.

I wondered if I should approach her. I remembered that she apparently was married, so I thought better about doing that.

I took a deep breath and kept talking to some of the people around the table. I so wanted to go over there and see her. After all, it seemed too coincidental that she was over there at the table, in the same bar, again. I wondered why she was continually put into my path, and I thought about what it was about her that made me feel compelled to get to know her.

"So, Ryan," Gina, a girl in accounting, was saying to me. "I'm really embarrassed to be asking you this, but I was wondering if you were, uh, seeing anybody."

Gina was a beautiful woman, no doubt about it, and very desirable. But I was totally distracted by Iris, who now looked like she wanted to bolt. I didn't blame her – she apparently had been stood up by somebody. Which gave me hope that maybe, just maybe, she wasn't the Iris who had gotten married all those months ago.

"Uh, Gina, I'm your boss. I'm not sure that I should go into my personal life right now. It would be entirely inappropriate to get involved with anybody at work."

"Oh, I know," she said. "I just thought it wouldn't hurt to ask." She looked completely embarrassed. "How about those Chiefs, huh?"

I smiled and looked over at Iris again. There was no doubt about it – she was waiting for somebody to show up, and this person evidently hadn't, thus far.

Then she caught my eye. I smiled and raised my glass and she immediately looked away.

I felt daunted. I had no idea if she was shy or was simply not interested. And, all at once, *I* was the one who was feeling shy.

Me, shy? What was the world coming to? But that was how I was feeling. Apprehensive about approaching her.

I caught her looking my way again and I smiled again. She looked around, as if she was trying to see who I was smiling at, and then looked away again. She put her hand on her forehead as if she was embarrassed and kind of scrunched down in her chair.

I took a deep breath and drank my scotch. A gorgeous woman, whom I didn't know, came and sat down right next to me.

"Hi," she said. "My name is Sandra. I couldn't help but notice you here. I think that you're the most stunning man I've ever seen."

I chuckled to myself, thinking that I had to hand it women like Sandra. They certainly didn't lack the confidence to say exactly what they are thinking. "Thanks," I said to her. "Hey, maybe I'll catch you around here, huh? I'm hanging with my co-workers tonight."

She looked a little stunned that I would be turning her down. I would imagine she wasn't used to such a thing. "Yes, well, I'll be around here for a little while longer. Come find me, maybe we can share a drink or something."

I nodded. "Sure. I'll be right on that." Then I realized that this sounded shittier than I intended, so I smiled and nodded my head at her. "Thanks for coming over, Sandra."

Sandra left, and I scanned the crowd. More and more people were streaming through the door, and I lost track of where Iris was. She didn't seem to be around anymore, or, at least, she wasn't in the same seat as she was before.

I looked at the bar, and there she was, having managed to snag one of the few available seats. She looked like she had been downing shots, as she had one in front of her, and several empty shot glasses next to her at the bar. People were jostling her, attempting to get the attention of the bartender, and she looked slightly annoyed.

But, mainly, she just looked lost. My heart went out to her.

She looked over at me briefly and then finally gave me a tentative smile. Then she looked around her again, as if she was trying to figure out if I was looking at her or somebody else.

I got up out of my seat, as I made a plan to go to the restroom, and then go up and get a drink right where she was sitting and strike up a casual conversation with her.

Unfortunately, this plan was thwarted by Daniela, of all people. She had just come through the door as a part of a group of women, and she had spied me and headed on over.

"Ryan," she said, as she made her way over to my table. "What a pleasant surprise." She was with three other women who were Daniela clones, really – all of them super fit, with long hair, a gorgeous face, and dressed to the nines. "Ryan, I would like you to meet my girlfriends Rachel, Lily and Caitlyn."

I stood up and shook all of these women's hands as Daniela put her arm around my back. "Ryan," Rachel said. "I've heard so much about you." She made eyes at Daniela and nodded her head approvingly. "Daniela told me you were handsome, but I had no idea."

I felt embarrassed, but I smiled at Rachel, and then looked over at the bar. To my dismay, Iris was no longer there. I wondered where she went, and I scanned the crowd some more while Daniela and her friends were standing there.

I finally saw her, talking to a woman, and I mentally felt relieved. I realized how rude I was being to Daniela and her friends, though, so I immediately turned my attention back to them. "Well, thank you, Rachel," I said, trying not to be too flirtatious. "You're not so bad yourself."

The other two girls made their introductions while Daniela stood right next to me with her arm around my back. I wondered how I was going to give her the slip. I only knew I had to. I felt this was my chance to find out more about this mystery woman.

This was going to be difficult, though, and would require some kind of finesse. Then I started to feel just a little bit uncomfortable – if Daniela was here, what if Erica and Brigitte were also around? My lifestyle was suddenly complicating my life. I had these women that I was having fun with, all of whom were indicating, more and more, that they were seeing me as something serious, all of whom might show up at that bar that evening.

That would be just my luck.

I wondered how Nick would handle just such a scenario. He was generally the manwhore, not me, although I definitely had my moments when I was in college.

I took a deep breath. Daniela was evidently waiting for me to introduce her to my co-workers, who were having a great time talking amongst themselves, drinking shots and eating appetizers. I knew she wanted to join us, too.

"Uh, Daniela," I said to her. "Where are you guys going to be? I'll catch up with you guys in a little bit. Would that be okay? This is kind of my first Happy Hour with the bank people, and, you know, they expect me to partake in the festivities of course."

"Oh, of course," she said, evidently hurt that I hadn't extended an invitation for her to join us. "We're going to try to grab a table outside. You better come and see me, though," she said with a smile. "I'll definitely make it worth your while." At that, she raised her eyebrows and I got her meaning. One thing about Daniela – she was gorgeous and good in bed.

But that wasn't what I was after that evening. I had to find a way to talk to Iris before she left. As it was, I was afraid she was going to leave. She seemed to be waiting for a date who didn't show. It would only be a matter of time until she figured out this guy wasn't showing, and she would disappear into the night.

Daniela disappeared, presumably to find a table on the patio outside, and I breathed a sigh of relief. Scanning the crowd, I saw Iris again. She was back at the bar, standing there, as there weren't any seats available. She was also apparently back to downing shots.

I stood up again, and, to my surprise, Iris appeared to be making her way over to my table. I caught her eye, and she was looking right at me. She appeared tentative, though, like she was completely unsure of what she was doing. I saw her looking around, and she walked extremely slowly. Her face also happened to be beet red.

I felt a twinge of excitement building as she slowly and tentatively made her way to my table. I looked right at her, so she didn't lose courage, and, at long last, she was standing right in front of me.

I felt my heart pounding as I smiled at her. I saw her take a deep breath and swallow hard. She ran her hand through her hair and straightened her clothes.

"Um, hi," she said, sounding like she had rehearsed what she was going to say to me. "I've seen you catching my eye a few times, and I feel totally stupid in coming over here, but, hi. I'm Iris."

I immediately felt charmed at her awkwardness. She didn't even try to come off smooth and confident. She reminded me of a 13-year-old girl at a party who was asking a boy to dance with her for the first time.

"Ryan," I said, holding out my hand for her to shake.

She was trembling wildly as she took my hand. "I'm so sorry," she said. "I don't usually come up to talk to guys like this, but…"

"No, no, I'm glad you came up to talk to me," I said. I could tell that she was extremely intoxicated, because her pupils were dilated and she was swaying. She was slurring her words as well. "Would you like to join us?" I pulled out a chair and motioned to it.

She shook her head. "No, no, that's okay. You're here with a bunch of people and I don't want to intrude."

I put my hand on the small of her back and I immediately felt the electricity from doing so. I leaned down to Renee, who was the closest person in proximity to me, and said "I'll be back in a bit. I'm going to try to find a table for me and Iris here."

She nodded, and I put my arm around Iris. "Let's try to find some other place to sit, shall we?"

She looked surprised that I would choose to leave my group so that I could talk to her. "Oh, you don't have to do that," she said.

"Well, they're probably going to want to leave soon anyhow. It's already 8, and we've all been here since around 5. So, I would imagine that the party soon will be breaking up."

She looked skeptical. "Okay, then."

I looked around the bar. It was just the right time – the Happy Hour crowds were clearing out, and the late night crowd hadn't yet arrived. The bar was still packed, but there were a few seats here and there. I made a beeline to a booth in a more secluded part of the bar.

"Let's go over here," I said. "I can't hear myself think in there."

She smiled and sat down across from me. I found that I wanted her to sit right next to me, which was odd, because I never had a woman sit next to me in a booth if there was nobody else at the table.

"I'm sorry," she said again. "I feel bad taking you away from your friends over there."

"Well, you know how it is. You go out with your co-workers and they start getting hammered. It's fun, but it gets old, too."

"Yes," she said. She looked like she couldn't quite believe she was talking to me.

I immediately looked at her ring finger. I didn't see a ring there, or any evidence of there ever being a ring, so I felt emboldened. "I know this is going to sound forward," I said. "But are you married?"

She burst out laughing. "I'm about as far from being married as you could possibly imagine. No. Not married. No children, either, unless you count my cat, Madison."

I breathed a sigh of relief.

She looked confused on why I was looking relieved. "I was wondering, I mean I guess you probably should ask that to a girl you just met in a bar, but why did you ask me that?" She was still nervous, because she was rambling just a little bit and her sentences were just a tad incoherent.

I smiled. "I don't know. I just thought you might be married."

She narrowed her eyes. A waitress came around and took our orders, and I ordered a neat scotch while she ordered a dirty martini. "I think I know you. I can't help but think you look familiar to me somehow."

I shrugged and tried to act nonchalant. Inside, though, I was feeling nervous and excited, two feelings I didn't think was possible to feel around a woman. "I don't know. Maybe you've seen me around downtown." I sipped my drink and pretended not to know anything about her. "What do you do? Do you work downtown? If so, maybe we've seen one another a time or two."

She nodded her head. "Yes, well, I used to work downtown. At the Public Defender's Office. But I don't anymore."

"The Public Defender's Office," I said. "What did you do there?"

"I was an attorney in the trial division," she explained. "But I didn't do that for very long. It wasn't for me – the long hours, the jail visits, the clients who had every excuse in the book. Not to mention the fact that I felt sorry for most of them." She smiled. "I've always rooted for the underdogs, which is what most of them were, at the heart of it."

She shut her mouth and looked around the room like she was embarrassed to be talking so much. "So, yeah, I used to work downtown. Now my office is out in Independence," she said, referring to the small city that was considered a suburb of Kansas City, "and I tend to stay out there with my cases." She took a breath. "And what do you do?"

"I'm a bank president," I said.

She smiled, and, again, gave me a look like she didn't quite think I was real. "Oh, okay," she said, and then looked down at her drink. I could see her face was getting even redder.

I smiled. "Why do you say it like that?"

"Nothing. I just…" She took a deep breath. "I have to tell you that I'm quite intoxicated, so I'm really sorry if I'm going to have some kind of diarrhea of the mouth." And then she giggled. "Oh, that sounds so gross. Anyhow, I don't think I've met anybody who looks like you and is so nice to boot. I feel like I'm dreaming." At that, she pinched her forearm. "I'm not, am I? Dreaming, I mean."

"No, not dreaming," I said. I wanted her to start feeling more relaxed, but she seemed anxious on top of being drunk. "So, tell me a little bit about yourself."

"Well, I…I don't know what to say, really. I'm an attorney, I have a cat, and I rescue pit bulls."

"You do? How long have you been doing that?"

"For several years. They're my favorite breed of dog, and I love them. I can't have a dog in my tiny apartment, though, so it gives me a chance to really be around something I really love." She took a deep breath. "Sometimes I think I love them more than most men I've met."

I laughed. She was certainly being honest, and it seemed that she was getting slightly more comfortable talking to me. I took that as a good sign, of course.

She bowed her head. "It's tragic, though, to be honest. I have a really difficult time sometimes rescuing them, because they haunt me. They end up with happy forever homes, but to know there are millions more who don't have that same happy story…" She had tears in her eyes. "Oh, sorry for getting so depressing with you. I'm sure you didn't come to this bar to meet a downer like myself."

"Oh, don't worry about that," I said. "I love that you spend your time rescuing dogs. I have a couple of mutts myself at home that I adopted from a shelter. Their names are Maximus and Brutus, and they really live up to their noble names."

She finally started to look like she was relaxing even

more. She said in a voice that was almost a whisper. "Are you, um, interested in me?" Her green eyes were getting wide.

"Yes, Iris, I'm definitely interested in you."

She cocked her head and took another sip of her drink. "I hope I remember all of this in the morning, although I probably won't." Then she smiled. "Liquid courage," she said, raising her glass. "That's really the only way I feel comfortable in places like this. Especially when I'm in a bar alone."

"You're here alone?" I asked her. I was curious about that – how she was there that evening. From watching her earlier, it evidently seemed she was waiting for somebody, but I couldn't be sure about that.

"Yes. You probably think I'm a dork for coming here alone, but I wasn't supposed to be. I was supposed to meet somebody here, but he didn't show."

"A blind date?"

"Yes." She looked sheepish. "A blind date. It was some guy I met on Tinder. You know how that is." Then she thought better of it. "Actually, you probably don't know how that is."

"Oh? You think that I don't meet people off Tinder?"

"No. A guy like you wouldn't have to. You would just attract women like moths to a flame."

I chuckled and took a sip of my scotch. "Would you like another one?" I asked her as the waiter came around.

"Please," she said.

I ordered for us. "Well," I said to Iris. "I'm glad that you think so highly of me, but I'm human." I didn't elaborate on that, though. She was right. I never did lack for female attention.

"So, what's your story? I don't see a wedding ring there, but I can't imagine you're not taken."

"I'm divorced. I've been divorced for several months now."

"Oh, I'm sorry," she said. "Divorce is tough. I know. I'm a sometime divorce lawyer. I mean sometime, because I try not to make that a major part of my practice. Too depressing and too much work for too little pay."

"Don't be sorry," I said. "Believe me, it was the best thing that could possibly happen."

"Oh? I know how that is. Although sometimes you don't know it when you're in it. You're involved in something toxic, but, when it goes away, you get really down anyhow. I think about that song about unanswered prayers sometimes – because I used to hope that some loser would keep me, but he didn't. There's an unanswered prayer right there, and thank God for that."

I smiled and realized that I wanted to go home with this woman. That night. There was something about her that was making me more turned on than I had ever felt before. With anybody.

I didn't want to be too forward, though, so I had to hang back a little bit. But I made a tentative gesture that made her know how I was feeling. I put my hand on her arm. She looked at it, and then looked at me. I could see that she was still feeling confused by our encounter. And that was okay. As long as she and I ended up together that night, all would be okay.

"Um," she said. "I…"

Just then, though, Daniela, of all people, found me. I groaned inwardly. Daniela, unfortunately, was the kind of woman who tended to intimidate other women. Especially women like Iris, who seemed none-too-confident about herself.

"Um, hello, Daniela," I said.

"I found you," she said to me. "I've been looking all over for you." She looked at Iris, then quizzically at me. She didn't look jealous or concerned, though. I would imagine that she probably thought Iris wasn't a threat because she wasn't a supermodel-type like Daniela was. "And who is this?"

"Daniela, this is Iris. Iris, Daniela."

"Hello," Iris said to the interloper Daniela. It was then that I noticed that Iris' words were slurred, more than I had noticed before. "It's good to meet you." At that, she looked unsure about whether or not she should stay there at the table with me. "Ryan, it's been good talking to you." She obviously could see that Daniela was into me, and she didn't want to come between us.

I stood up. I had no idea what I should do in that situation. Iris was obviously intimidated by Daniela, just as I thought she would be. And, really, I was dating Daniela, so blowing her off would be shitty of me.

At the same time, I knew I didn't want to lose contact with Iris. I already felt bonded to her and I just met her. I realized that the feelings I'd gotten before when I just saw her were real. I couldn't explain it, either. It was just one of those things.

I wondered about the concept of love at first sight, and if that were true. I never believed in that – lust at first sight, yeah. For sure. But love at first sight?

"Iris," I said. "Please stay here." I looked at Daniela, who now was giving me the stink eye. "I'm so sorry, Daniela. I'll have to catch up with you tomorrow or something. I hope that's okay?"

She crossed her arms in front of her, obviously not liking where this was going. "Sure," she said, although her face and body language told me this wasn't okay with her. At all. "Give me a call tomorrow. Or I'll call you. Maybe we can just hang out this weekend, huh?"

I nodded and said nothing. I didn't want Iris to get the wrong idea, but it was clear to me she was. She was looking confused again.

"See you later, Daniela," I said. Daniela was now flanked by her girlfriends. "And it was nice meeting all of you," I said, addressing the other women.

"You too," Rachel said, and the others said similar things.

And, just like that, the gaggle of women had left.

Iris looked bewildered. "Oh, I'm so embarrassed. You're dating that girl, aren't you?"

"Yeah." I tried not to meet her eyes, but I did. She didn't look upset, though, and I mentally made a note that this was a plus for her.

"Beautiful girl." And, at that, she looked again like she felt out of place. She gulped down some more of her drink. "Egads, I'm going to be paying for this tomorrow. I haven't drank like this since college, really." She looked anxious. "And I usually end up apologizing profusely to somebody when I wake up the next morning. Not that I always remember the night before, but I do usually end up doing something to apologize for."

"Relax," I said. "You're doing fine. There's been nothing so far you need to apologize for. I would tell you if there was."

"You would?"

"Yes, I would."

"You seem like such a nice guy. I don't know, I always

look at guys like you and say 'out of my league.' And the second thing I think is 'jerk.'" Then she started to laugh. "Oh, lord, I have to stop myself now. I'm saying way too much."

"You're okay. You're fine." I really did think that, too. There was something about her....

She shook her head. "Man. I think I'm going to have to call an Uber soon."

"Don't go," I said, perhaps too quickly. "I would really like to get to know you more."

"Okay," she said.

And then we talked. She drank some more, as well, but, for the next few hours, we talked about everything under the sun. She alternated between seeming like she was getting comfortable with me with seeming like she was nervous again. Not that I minded any of that. I just wanted to stay there with her. I wanted to get to know her.

And then, I admit, I wanted to get naked with her. I wanted that more than I thought I could possibly want anything in my life.

But I had to bide my time.

Finally, it was 2 AM, and the bar was closing. "Iris," I said, nervously. "What are you doing now? I mean, do you have any plans to meet anyone for breakfast or anything like that?" There were a few open all night diners where people gathered after the bars closed. I knew, however, even as I said the words, that she didn't have any place to go after the bar closed.

"No, of course not."

"I hope it's not too forward to ask you to go to a hotel with me?"

She smiled and looked suspicious. "Really? You and me?

In a hotel together?" She shook her head. "Not going to say no to that. Talk about a once in a lifetime opportunity."

And, at that, I paid the tab and the two of us headed out to the limousine that I had called to come and pick us up. Daniel was my new driver, and he was there right when I asked him to be.

I couldn't wait to be truly alone with this woman.

Chapter Twenty-Seven

I felt very nervous as the limo made its way to The Fontaine in the Country Club Plaza. I chose this place, as opposed to my own home, because it was close to where the bar was. I couldn't believe how anxious I was to be alone with this woman.

At the same time, I was apprehensive, because she was evidently pretty intoxicated. I really wanted to have sex with her, but I really didn't want to do that if she was so drunk that she didn't know what she was doing. Her eyes were unfocused and I could hear her breathing heavily right next to me.

"Iris," I said, putting my arm around her, "are you okay?"

"I am," she said. "I'm just a little bit in shock that I'm in a limo with a guy like you. Not that I think you're some kind of a freak or a serial killer or anything like that. Quite the opposite. I just can't believe that a guy like you would be taking a girl like me home. Or to a hotel room. Or wherever we're going." Then she giggled lightly, and I felt charmed by the lilting sound of her laugh.

Charmed, captivated and completely hard.

"Iris," I said to her, as I got closer to her in the limo. I could hear my own heart pounding in my chest. "Can I kiss you?"

She nodded and gulped. She was trembling a little bit as I put my hand on the back of her head and drew her in closer to me. I breathed in her scent, which was a combination of a sweet floral perfume, almond shampoo and peppermint gum.

It was strange, being so close to the woman that I had been thinking about for close to a year. Strange and titillating at the same time. Surprisingly, I felt myself feeling just a tad bit nervous. I wondered what would happen if I didn't feel it after kissing her. Would that mean my feelings all this time didn't mean anything? That maybe I was wrong?

I took a deep breath and gently put my lips on hers. As I felt my erection stiffen in my pants and my heart pound ever more fiercely, I knew it was right with her. That kiss solidified that I had, somehow, someway, fallen in love with this woman at first sight. I felt that kiss throughout my entire body, and I found that I actually had briefly lost my breath.

She responded to the kiss by throwing her arms around me and leaning in towards me even more. As her soft lips were at first gently pressing onto mine, and then more urgent, I had to stop myself from going further with her right there in the limo.

I finally broke away from her and looked into her eyes. They were huge and she looked like she didn't quite believe what was happening. "Am I dreaming?" she said to me. "I can't quite believe that a guy like you would be interested in a girl like me. Even when I'm this drunk."

I put my hand on her cheek. "Believe it. I am very inter-ested in you. I'm more interested in you than I think that I've ever been in any woman in my life. Which sounds crazy, because I have only just met you." I didn't mention to her about all the times that I saw her and that I couldn't stop thinking about her. She rightly would have thought I'd lost my mind. She might have thought that I was some kind of a stalker, and that was the last thing I wanted her to believe.

She shook her head. "Totally surreal." Then she took a deep breath. "I don't want you to think that I, you know, do this kind of thing. With just anybody, I mean. I don't. But I…"

I looked at her expectantly, but said nothing.

She continued. "I don't know how to explain this. But I feel like I know you. Like I've known you all my life. I know this sounds completely weird, and I'm sorry about that, but I think you're obviously a gorgeous, gorgeous man. You are, but, even so, there's so much more to you for me." Then she shook her head. "I'm so sorry. I always tend to blab so much when I've been drinking a lot. Embarrassing."

I just looked at her. "Don't be embarrassed, because I feel exactly the same way about you. Like I've known you all my life."

She gulped. "Where are we going?"

"To The Fontaine. On the Plaza. It's a beautiful space. I'm so sorry, I would take you home, but I live in Leawood. In the Hallbrook Area. That's just a little far away. I mean, it's not that far away – it's only about twenty minutes from here. But I hope that I'm not too forward when I tell you I don't want to wait that long."

At that, I kissed her again. I felt strongly that I had to do that. I felt compelled to kiss her. Like she had some kind of a strong pull for me. I felt helpless to fight against the feeling I was having just being near her.

The limo pulled up to the hotel, and we got out. I arranged a suite for us, and the two of us went up the elevator. To the room.

We got into the room, and I found myself even more nervous. I had no idea why. This wasn't the first time that I had brought a woman that I had just met to a hotel room. Not by a long shot. But this was different. Way different. I couldn't explain it if I tried, but I felt so connected to this woman, I knew that she and I were somehow on a path that would lead to something amazing.

We sat down on the couch, and I decided that I just needed to put aside my nervousness and just go for what I needed and wanted to do.

I kissed her, and then I gently put my hand on her breast. She sighed as I deftly removed her bra while I kissed her neck. Her face was getting red, but she was breathing hard and moaning a little bit.

"Your skin feels amazing," I said, trying hard to tamp down my raging hard-on. Not that I didn't want to have a hard-on, but I knew that I didn't want to get too excited too quickly. I wanted to go slowly with her. To make love to her like I hadn't ever made love to anyone in my life. All my life, I had met women I didn't really care about, as far as long-term. The exception to that, of course, was Alexis, but I didn't think I was ever really in love with her.

With one shaking hand, she unbuttoned my shirt. As her smooth hands ran all over my body, I felt her tender touch to my very core. "You're warm," she said, as she looked at my chest and stomach appreciatively. "And you're so beautiful. I don't think I've ever seen anybody this perfect in my entire life."

I felt myself blushing, in spite of myself. She was so cute, and what made her beautiful in my eyes was that she obviously had no idea how cute she was. She was really the opposite of the kind of women I'd gone for in my life – Iris was unsure of herself and seemed to be very kind and gentle. All of the women I had gone for before were generally picture perfect and knew it.

"I think you're beautiful, too," I said to her.

She shook her head. "No, no, I'm not," she said. "I mean, thank you for saying that, but I…"

I put my finger over her mouth. "You are. You are beautiful. Don't ever say you're not, because you are."

She took a deep breath. Her eyes brimmed with tears and she shook her head. "Thank you for saying that."

"I'm not just saying that. I mean it."

She smiled and nervously put her hands on my back as I leaned a little closer to her. I ran my hands through her thick hair, and she bent her head while I did this. She moaned a little as I slowly and casually put my hands on her stomach. At first, she looked like she was self-conscious about this, but she soon got into it, as her breathing started coming faster and heavier. She laid back on the couch as I put my hands on her breasts and stomach.

I lifted her shirt off of her, and I gently licked her abs and made my way up to her breasts. I watched the reaction on her face as to whether or not she was enjoying it, and I could tell she was. She no longer had a look of being unsure, but, rather, she was smiling and she had a look of complete ecstasy on her face.

She pulled my hair and brought my face up to hers, while she spread her legs and wrapped them around me. I looked into her eyes, and then kissed her long and deep. I lay down almost on top of her, but my weight wasn't on her completely. By this time, both of us were breathing heavily and I could hear her heart, which was pounding as loudly as my own.

She was still wearing her skirt and her shoes, so I took off her shoes. She giggled a little. "Those are my Jimmy Choos," she said proudly. I kind of knew my designers, so I understood that she paid a pretty penny for the shoes. That was probably why she seemed so proud about them - it didn't seem that she was particularly wealthy. Not that this mattered to me at all.

I smiled as I pulled off her skirt. She lifted her body off of the couch as I did so. Then I tentatively fingered her clit, and she moaned. She nodded her head. "Yes, do it. Please do it."

I put my head between her legs and gently stimulated her clit with my tongue. She bucked up a little off the couch and started to moan louder than before. I put my hands under her rear and I massaged them gently while I continued to lick her clit and thrust my tongue inside of her.

"Oh, that feels amazing. You do that so well." I knew that she was enjoying herself, because her head was shaking and her breathing was heavy.

At some point, she sat up and nervously unbuckled my belt and my pants. She stroked my cock through my underwear, and I could feel it getting harder and harder. She then brought it out, and she gasped a little as she stared at it. "Wow," she said, as her hand flew up to her mouth. Her eyes got wide. "I haven't done this in awhile, and you're...." She drew a breath. "I don't think I've seen anything quite like this."

And then she giggled. I laughed as well.

Then she looked like she was summoning her determination, and proceeded to put her lips around my throbbing penis. I groaned and tried mightily to hold back, but it was difficult – she was very good at this. Very good at it. She licked, sucked and lightly bit me while her hands played gently with my balls. She also gently teased my ass with her fingers. I was surprised that she would feel comfortable enough to go there, but she was deft at this, and I, once again, had to hold myself back from coming.

Then, she was finished with this, and she climbed on top of me. I put my hand behind her head and I just kissed her for what seemed forever. As I kissed her, I put my hands on her breasts and ran my fingers through her hair.

She pulled away from me briefly and looked unsure of herself again. "Would you like to…" And then she motioned her head over to the king-sized bed.

"I would very much like to," I said to her. Then I picked her up and carried her over to the bed and laid her down on it gently.

I lay down next to her and stroked her body. Then I kissed her. "I have a condom," she said to me, her face getting red. "I guess I was hopeful, but I had no idea that I would meet somebody like you." She shook her head. "This still seems totally surreal to me." At that, she took a condom out of her purse.

I sheathed my raging hard-on and I gently entered her. She gasped as I slowly filled her up. "Are you okay?" I asked her.

She nodded her head rapidly. "More than okay. This feels amazing." She put her hands behind my head and I lowered my head to hers. I kissed her gently, full on the mouth, and she closed her eyes as I rhythmically glided in and out of her. She was tight, so tight. I could tell that she was right about not having sex in a long time.

She rocked underneath me, and she pushed me onto the bed and got on top of me. As she rode me, she pressed her breasts against my torso and buried her head in my neck. I kissed her cheeks and forehead, and then lightly bit her lips. She nibbled on my earlobes and ran her hands through my hair. "Oh my God, you're just so gorgeous," she said between her breaths, which were coming on heavier and heavier.

I finally came, and she seemed to as well. She was shaking all over. I reached for a glass of water and gave it to her. "Here," I said. "I think you might be needing this."

She nodded her head. "I do. More than you know." She looked at me, her green eyes searching my face. "Thank you. Thank you for a wonderful night and making me feel special. That isn't a feeling I'm used to."

My heart went out to her when she said that. I put my hand on her cheek and stroked it lightly. "You should feel special. I'm happy to make you feel that way."

She lay down on the pillow, and gripped it tightly. And then her eyes closed and, with a small smile, she seemed to completely conk out.

I stayed up for another few hours and just watched her sleeping. As I did so, I wondered about that evening. How I felt so strongly for her when I didn't know her. I just met her. I had no idea how I had come so far with my feelings for this enigmatic woman. I only knew that I did, and I didn't have any desire to leave her side.

I FINALLY FELL ASLEEP about five in the morning. I was restless that entire evening. I wanted so much to keep touching her, keep making love to her. But I didn't want to wake her up, either, so I just let her sleep while I lay beside her. I reveled in the sound of her breathing and in the sounds she made in her sleep.

I fell asleep with my arms wrapped around her.

But in the morning, I woke up to find that she was gone. She didn't even leave a note.

Chapter Twenty-Eight

When I woke up and found that she wasn't around, at first I was really upset. I felt as if I had finally found the woman who was going to make me happy, and she obviously didn't feel the same way about me.

But, at the same time, I knew that there was no way I was going to give up that quickly. I finally found her, and making love with her gave me a feeling that I hadn't had before.

Perhaps she wasn't feeling it. I hoped and prayed that wasn't the case.

I knew in my gut, however, that she *was* feeling it. So, it had to be something else. She probably was embarrassed. Or maybe she was drunker than I thought. I knew the feeling of waking up after drinking way too much the previous night, and not knowing where I was. The feeling that I always got in those situations was one of needing to get away as quickly as possible.

I couldn't take it personally that she had left without a word.

Nick, of course, didn't help the situation any. He called me, wanting to know if I wanted to get a drink that evening.

"Yeah," I said to him. "That's sounds great." I actually was anxious to talk to him and get his take on the Iris thing. I felt like a girl, wanting to tell my best friend all about the new person I met.

The new person I met and let slip through my fingers. I kicked myself for being such a sound sleeper that I didn't wake up and stop her before she left.

I MET NICK FOR A DRINK THAT EVENING. He took one look at me and said "you look different, buddy. I don't think that I've seen you look this relaxed, ever. What gives?"

"I met her. The One."

He chuckled. "What the hell are you talking about? I spoke to you yesterday afternoon, and you were still dating those three women that you couldn't give two craps about. Now you're telling me that you met The One? Don't you think that's just a little bit premature there, Ryan?"

"I didn't think that you would understand," I said.

"Oh, wait. The redhead?"

"Yes." I took a deep breath as he looked at me skeptically. "But there's one problem."

"What's that?"

"We went to a hotel room last night. We…."

"Did the dirty on the first night. Nice," Nick said approvingly.

"I was going to say made love. Anyhow, it was spectacular. That's the only thing that I can say about it. But I woke up and she was gone."

Nick shook his head. "That sucks. What are you going to do about that?"

"Find her, obviously. But I wanted to get your opinion on it. What would you do in this situation?"

"Oh, come on, you know what I would do. I'd be thanking my lucky stars that I wouldn't have to see her again. You know that I've fucked women I've met in bars and it rarely turns out good. They've always come back to haunt me. And you, too. You've had your share of stalkers in your life. So, if she just left you there in the hotel room without a word, consider it a blessing. You've dodged a bullet."

I took a deep breath. "I'm sorry I asked this question to you. I knew you wouldn't understand."

Nick shook his head. "Okay, well, this woman obviously means something to you. For whatever reason. As I said, it shows on your face that you've changed for the better. You actually look…peaceful. I guess that's the best way I can describe it. So, try to find her."

"Easier said than done. I have no idea where to start. I could go back to where she used to work, but they're pretty tight-lipped about giving out information about her. Which I don't blame them for, by the way – she was a Public Defender. I would imagine that stalkers might be a problem in that line of work. But that's probably where I'm going to start as far as finding her again."

"Well, I wish you luck," he said. "And I hate to ask this, but I guess I should. What about Daniela? And, for that matter, Brigitte and Erica?"

"I think it goes without saying that I'm going to stop seeing them."

"You're nuts. You just met this Iris woman. You're dating three of the most beautiful women on the planet, and all of them are crazy about you. Crazy about you. I would strongly urge you against dumping them just because this Iris woman has come on the scene."

"Nick, at some point, I have to settle down. And, I don't know, it just feels right with Iris. I don't expect you to understand, though, because I don't think that you've experienced something like this. When I was talking to her last night, I felt like I'd always known her. She said similar things to me. Until something like this happens to you, I don't think that you can really see things the same way I do."

He shook his head. "Whatever. I would keep those women as insurance policies, if you ask me. Especially since you don't even know if you're going to be able to see Iris again."

I looked at him for a beat, and suddenly understood what was at the bottom of him dissuading me from Iris. "Nick, how are things going with Rielle?" I asked him.

"Shitty. Why?"

I subtly put my hand on his knee. "I have this feeling that perhaps you're jealous. You don't want me to really settle down because you and I won't be able to get together anymore. And I don't mean hang out – we'll always hang out. But you and I won't be able to…" Then I motioned with my hands so that he understood what I meant.

"Yeah, I admit, I'll miss that. So maybe that's part of it. But mainly I just think that you're acting rash, just like you always have with Alexis. You don't know this Iris. She could be Alexis 2.0 for all you know. I just don't want to see you get sucked in, yet again, by a nutty bitch."

"I'll take that chance."

"Well, go for it. Far be it for me to try to tell you what to do. But, please, for the love of all that's holy, don't dump the other women just yet. See if Iris is worth it first."

I nodded, but made a mental note that I wasn't going to

listen to him. I wanted to be with Iris and that, really, was that.

AFTER I GOT HOME AFTER HAVING DRINKS WITH NICK, I looked around the house and felt lonelier than ever. I was really happy that Maximus and Brutus were around, because they always made me feel good. But I really wanted a woman to be around this house on a permanent basis.

I wanted Iris to be that woman.

I sighed, and went upstairs. My jacket that I had brought to the bar was on a chair, and I was going to hang it up. I made a mental note to take it to the dry cleaner, so I checked the pockets.

And my heart stopped.

In the pocket of the jacket was one of Iris' business cards!

Just like that, I knew I was going to see her again.

And I couldn't be more excited about it.

Chapter Twenty-Nine

I couldn't be more nervous as I made my way to Iris' law office on the Independence Square. It was in a modest brick building that was about two stories tall. Her suite was just as modest. I entered the suite and was greeted by a young woman with blue hair in the front, reddish hair everywhere else. She surprisingly carried it off quite well.

She looked at me as if she didn't quite understand why I was there. "Can I help you?" she asked me.

"Yes. I'm here to see Iris Snowe."

She nodded. "She isn't here at the moment. She's in court. But let me know what you're selling and be sure to leave your business card, and I'll ask her to give you a call when she gets in."

I took a deep breath. "I'm not here to sell her anything," I said.

She looked perplexed. "Okay....I'm so sorry, I don't have you down on my schedule to talk to her about your legal problems." And then she looked at her calendar on her computer. "Iris doesn't have any afternoon appointments, though, so you can probably talk to her when she gets in."

I opened my mouth to tell her that I wasn't there as a client, either, but thought better of it. I had no idea what it was that I was going to say. "I hope you don't mind if I wait for Iris to get into the office," I said.

"No, of course not. Can I offer you some water?"

"Sure," I said, and then sat down on the red velour couch.

The girl got some water for me, and I picked up one of the magazines that was on the coffee table in front of me. I flipped through it and patiently sipped my water. I wanted to ask her when Iris would be back in the office, but I didn't want to sound pushy.

IRIS APPEARED IN THE OFFICE about a half hour later, and I could tell when she looked at me that she didn't remember who I was.

I briefly felt humiliated as I realized that she had forgotten me, but my second thought was shame that I had sex with her. I had no idea that she was that drunk. If I had known that she was drunk enough that she wouldn't have remembered the entire evening, I would have been more of a gentleman than that.

"Hi," she said, holding out her hand. "May I help you?"

My heart sunk just a little and I nervously ran my hand through my hair. Daunted, I simply told her that I was there to see her.

She looked quizzical as she said "oh, okay. My office is right here." She gestured towards a smallish office that was connected to the waiting room.

I went into the office with her and noticed that there

were files piled up everywhere on the desk. She hastily put them on the floor and faced me. The look on her face was one of being perplexed, yet I noticed there was also intrigue in those eyes of hers.

"You really don't remember me, do you?" I said to her. Inwardly, I was feeling completely humiliated and was questioning my connection to her. I mean, I wasn't exactly questioning that *I* felt connected to her. Rather, I was seriously questioning that *she* felt the same way about *me*. How could she, when she didn't even remember me?

When I asked her if she remembered me, her face got red and I could tell, in her eyes, that she really didn't.

I took a deep breath, realizing my first hunch was probably correct – she was completely wasted the other night. Much moreso than I ever could have imagined. I felt that I had taken advantage of a drunk woman, and this embarrassed me further. Still, I had to press on. I felt compelled to, even though my ego was extremely bruised. Maybe even my heart was bruised by this point.

"I'm really embarrassed," I began, and that was the gods-honest truth. "I guess I didn't know you were that drunk the other night."

At that point, I started to see a light come into her eyes. A light of recognition. The "ah ha" moment. Yet, she still tried to hedge her bets. "I'm so sorry. I don't know what you mean."

I could see her starting to come around, so I decided to lighten things up a bit. "Harry's Bar. You and I doing shots together. Any of this ringing a bell?"

All at once, the light I saw in her eyes was becoming brighter. She smiled shyly, and I felt captivated again. "Um, did any of those shots happen to be te-killya," she asked.

I chuckled. Tequila was my bane as well. "A few."

And, just like that, she looked ashamed, and I felt bad. She lowered her head and put her hands over eyes. I could see that there were small tears that had formed. So, I smiled encouragingly and felt slightly charmed by the redness forming on her cheeks.

"Gosh, I'm so embarrassed. Um, I didn't act a fool, did I?" she asked, her eyes now getting wide. The redness that had formed on her cheeks was spreading across her entire face.

"Not at all," I said, trying desperately to reassure her. I could tell that she really didn't think much of herself, and, for some odd reason, that made her even more appealing to me. I had my share of women who thought that they were "all that," and look where that got me. I liked that she was modest and a bit shy. "You came up to me, and before I knew it, we were chatting like we were old friends. We talked for hours about everything from liberal politics to Oscar Wilde. I was quite impressed with your knowledge of *The Importance of Being Ernest.* I think we even talked about the Kardashians."

At that, she smiled and looked just a little bit dumb-founded. She did seem that she was coming around, though, so I felt emboldened.

"Uh, I think I owe you an apology," I said, intending to apologize for taking advantage of her.

She raised an eyebrow and cocked her head. "For what?" she asked, suppressing a smile. I was happy that she seemed much more relaxed, so I also relaxed.

"If I would have known you were that, uh…."

"Smashed?" she said, her sly smile becoming more prominent.

"Yeah. Well, I wouldn't have…"

"Taken me to a hotel room and torn my clothes off?" she said with a slight giggle.

"Yeah." I, too, was suppressing a smile. And I was noticing that, as she was gradually becoming more comfortable around me, she seemed to really glow. I knew then that I had done the right thing is tracking her down. I could see in her face that she was attracted to me, just as much as she had shown the previous evening at the bar.

So, I took courage in the change in her demeanor and decided to just go for it and ask her out. "So I was wondering…" I trailed off, suddenly feeling just a little bit shy. I had no idea why. I guess I was afraid of being shot down, which was an odd feeling for me. I had never in my life been afraid of being shot down, mainly because, well, I had never in my life been shot down. "I was wondering if you would be interested in having drinks with me sometime."

After I said this, I realized that I was holding my breath while I waited for her answer to this question.

She took a deep breath and simply said "sure."

So, we made a date. We agreed to meet up at Harry's, with her making a joke about the two of us returning to the scene of the crime. I found it cute that she said this, because it showed that she was actually relaxing around me.

I left her office singing a song under my breath. I had to get to work, but I thought about her the entire way to my office.

And couldn't take my mind off of her for the rest of the day.

Friday couldn't get here fast enough.

Beautiful Illusions: Chapter One

IRIS

I woke up in a strange hotel room. Cotton mouth, a strange, sweet taste on my tongue, a feeling that every muscle was bloated and filled with liquid. My head was pounding, my hands shaking. My hair hurt, and the light streaming through the window was just.too.bright. I attempted to run one hand through my hair, but the hand was caught in a massive tangle. I pulled on my hair and then gave up. The tangle wasn't going to come out. I felt nauseated, and the sensation that came over me was that I was about to hurl. I swallowed hard several times until the feeling passed. I had no idea where the bathroom was, and the last thing I wanted to do was throw up in the bed. Where was I? And who was this guy in this bed? A head of dark hair, but the body was covered in a sheet. He was breathing heavily, evidently knocked cold.

I surreptitiously snuck out of bed, hoping my clothes were around somewhere. On tip-toe, I prowled around the room. It was a very nice room. A suite, in fact. I didn't have time to look around. I had to get out of there. I got on my hands and knees, looking under the bed. Nothing was there. I crawled around the room, becoming frantic at the prospect of being unable to find my clothes. I finally got up and tip-toed out of the room and into the next room.

Through bleary eyes, my head pounding like a Stewart Copeland drum solo, I finally saw my clothes in a pile. My precious red Mary Jane Jimmy Choos, which I spent way too much on, were next to the white sofa. My skirt and shirt were next to them.

I breathed a sigh of relief.

I looked at my hand, which was shaking. I didn't know if I was shaking because of the situation or the effects of the hangover.

Probably both.

I got dressed and then realized I had no idea where my purse was. Panic started anew in my throat. By now, I was beginning to understand that this particular suite was gorgeous. Modern art on the walls and the furniture was modern as well. Distinctively modern. Soft white leather, chrome feet. Marble coffee table in front. Enormous flat-screen TV. There were orchids on a glass table by the window.

This guy certainly had taste.

Just then, I heard my ringtone. Radiohead's *Creep*. It was across the room, and I shot over to my purse. My ringtone was so fucking loud! I immediately silenced it. But the phone helped me find my purse, so there was that.

Then I crept out the door, shutting it gently behind me.

In the cab on the way home, I tried to piece it all together.

Where was I? I was doing shots in a bar. Happy Hour. I met a guy last night. Obviously. I couldn't remember much about him. I couldn't pick him out of a lineup at this point.

You're too old for this shit. It had been a good five years since I was in college, and college was the last time I had this kind of slutty one-night stand. I didn't remember why I started drinking so much. My thoughts were hazy, and I felt exhausted like every cell in my body was filled with alcohol.

Let me see...I was going to meet a guy off the internet. That didn't pan out. Of course. The dude didn't show. And I...went up to a guy and started chatting with him. Which was totally like me. When I'm drinking, anyhow. Otherwise, I'm painfully shy and insecure about myself.

I only remembered a few details. Most things were a blur.

I examined my phone, holding my breath. *Please, please, please let there be no dialed calls late last night.* Shaking, I looked through my log of dialed calls. Drunk-dialing would be just like me. There should be an invention where the phone can tell if you've had a few too many and prevent you from calling anybody.

Nothing was on the dialed calls log.

I sighed in relief.

Then I just sighed.

I'm too old for this shit.

I looked again at the call log to see who'd called me this morning. It was my best friend, Debbie. I called a cab, then called her on my drive home.

"Yeah," I said. "What's up?"

"Hey there, girlfriend, how you doing?"

"Great, great." Or, I would be doing great if I didn't have the overwhelming feeling I was about to hurl. The motion of the cab was literally making me gag.

This was going to be a long cab ride home.

"Oh, I did something really stupid," I said.

"What's that?"

"I met somebody and went home with him. I just got done taking the walk of shame, and I'm in the cab right now."

"Awesome," she said. "You need to get laid. How long has it been?"

"Since the early stone age," I said. "At least. One thing, though."

"What's that?"

"I don't remember any of it. I have no idea who was in the bed next to me this morning." *Oh, God, this is so embarrassing*.

"So, what're you doing now?"

"I gotta pit bull rescue to do. I really don't feel like it. I just want to go home and go to bed. And puke. I need to seriously puke. But that dog needs me, so I gotta go."

"That's too bad. I was calling to see if you wanted to have lunch somewhere."

"Maybe tomorrow. Sunday brunch, maybe."

"Sure, let's meet for brunch."

We decided to meet at a restaurant that was central to both of us. It was a place that served a hearty brunch buffet. Right at that moment, though, any kind of food sounded unappetizing, to say the very least.

I went home, made myself throw up, changed, and then went to the abandoned house where a pit bull was left in the basement after the owners were foreclosed. It was scary how many of these calls we got. I went to the house, permit to enter in hand, opened the door and went downstairs. There was a 9-month-old puppy down there, whining and barking. When she saw me, her entire little body squirmed with delight. I kneeled down, and she licked me on the face profusely. I had a bag of food, a jug of water and a bowl, and I fed her and gave her the water. She wolfed down the food, looked to me for more, and gulped the water.

"There, there, my little one," I said. "That's all you can have for now, but you'll get more in the shelter, I promise." She licked me some more as I unchained her, leashed her, put her in my car, and took her to a shelter. I had a large carrier in the car, and I could hear her whining.

I prayed she'd find a forever home quickly.

Pit bulls really are the sweetest dogs.

After my rescue mission, I headed home and passed out on the couch.

Oh, I'm never drinking again.

Beautiful Illusions: Chapter Two

On Monday morning, I arrived at my law office, where my assistant greeted me. Melinda had hair that was variously blue or green in the front, and when I called her, I was subjected to a Ramones song. I didn't generally dig the Ramones. The Sex Pistols, maybe, but not the Ramones. Still, she was fun, cool and efficient. Everybody loved her, including me.

I noticed a guy sitting on the couch in my peripheral vision. I was surprised to find out I had somebody coming in.

I looked quizzically at Melinda.

She motioned me to come a little closer. I bent my head down, then she said in a low voice, "this guy's here to see you."

I looked at the man, and my heart quickened. He was the most beautiful man I had ever seen. In.my.life. Thick dark hair. Eyes greener than I'd ever seen. He looked at me, an impish smile on his chiseled face, and when he smiled, I noticed his teeth were perfect like he spent his entire

213

younger years in braces. He was wearing an expensive-looking tailor-made grey suit with a silk shirt underneath. Italian shoes.

I wondered why he'd be in my office. He definitely didn't look the type who'd be slumming with a bargain-basement divorce lawyer like myself or filing for personal bankruptcy. Those were my two major areas of practice. I also did some criminal law, and he certainly didn't look like the kind of guy who'd need a criminal attorney. Well, maybe a white-collar criminal attorney, but those are the bigwigs in the high rises. I was as far from a bigwig as you could possibly imagine.

At the same time, he looked so familiar....

No. It couldn't be.

Beautiful man stood up and smiled broadly.

Tentatively, I said, "Hello. Can I help you?"

His smile disappeared. He ran one of his hands through his thick mane of dark hair, his head slightly cocked down, his mesmerizing eyes looking at me questioningly.

I drew a breath.

His face turned red. "Uh, I'm here to see you."

"Oh, ok, sure. My office is right there," I said, pointing to the door.

What the hell?

He followed me in. Files were piled on the desk, on the floor, and on top of the computer.

"Sorry about that," I said, frantically taking the piles on the desk and throwing them to the floor behind me. I was suddenly nervous and had no real idea why. This guy was magnetic, so he made me nervous, but it was more than that. I couldn't quite place him, but my subconscious mind knew exactly who he was.

My subconscious just refused to communicate with me at the moment.

"Have a seat."

He sat down on the red tweed chair. My office was small, about 10 x 10, which was all I could afford. Although I was an attorney, I definitely wasn't highly paid. I spent most of my time worrying about people who didn't pay their bills and chasing after them. Plus, my student loans from 7 years of schooling were choking the life out of me.

He still had a quizzical look in those beautiful green eyes.

Then he began. "You don't remember me, do you?"

I bit my lip and raised my eyebrows in an expression that said, "No, sorry."

He looked down. "I'm really embarrassed. I didn't know you were that drunk the other night."

At this point, I could feel my heart in my throat. No. It couldn't be. Never in a million years would I end up with somebody who looked like him. Never.

I must've been on some kind of candid camera show. There was a Canadian show called *Just for Laughs,* where actors played pranks on unsuspecting people and filmed their reactions. This was probably what this was, although I wasn't aware that there was an American version.

I took a deep breath, not wanting to jump to conclusions, and said, "I'm so sorry. I don't know what you mean."

"Harry's Bar. You and I doing shots together. Any of this ringing a bell?"

It was my turn to be embarrassed. Actually, it should've been my turn to be embarrassed when I first saw him. It was now becoming clear, but I didn't think I'd ever catch the eye of a guy like this.

And I didn't think I'd ever see my hotel mystery man again.

"Um, did any of those shots happen to be te-killya?" I asked.

He smiled. "A few."

I felt tears coming to my eyes. I had no idea why. I lowered my head, putting it in my hands, and then peeked through my hands at him.

He was smiling again, and I was completely captivated. God, this guy could completely light up a pitch-black room. Just the same, ending up with him was a lucky shot on my part that no doubt included beer goggles for him. I was halfway decent looking and could lose a few pounds, but this guy belonged with a Giselle Bundchen clone.

"Gosh, I'm so embarrassed. I didn't act a fool, did I?" Of course I did. I usually did act a fool after tequila.

"Not at all. You came up to me, and before I knew it, we were chatting like old friends. We talked for hours about everything from liberal politics to Oscar Wilde. I was quite impressed with your knowledge of *The Importance of Being Earnest*." He paused. "I think we even talked about the Kardashians."

The Importance of Being Earnest. I read that play after seeing the movie. But I wondered why I'd be talking about that. Still, it was impressive for me to find somebody who even knew who Oscar Wilde was. I couldn't count how many times I'd met a guy who thought Tennessee Williams was a country singer.

He was looking embarrassed again. "I think I owe you an apology."

I raised an eyebrow and cocked my head slightly. "For what?"

"If I would've known you were that, uh..."

"Smashed?" I said helpfully.

"Yeah. Well, I wouldn't have..."

"Taken me to a hotel room and torn my clothes off?" This was like a mad libs game.

"Yeah."

Oh, the irony. I ended up with a jaw-droppingly beautiful man who was literate, and I didn't even have a good memory of it. I hoped I enjoyed it at the time.

Didn't matter. If I didn't remember it, it didn't really happen. In my mind, at least.

Then it struck me. Why was he here? And how did he find me? The only thing I could think of was I left something in the hotel room, and he was enough of a gentleman to return it to me. But I couldn't imagine what I left there.

I realized something else. This guy was intimidatingly beautiful, yet I felt completely comfortable with him. Mesmerized, captivated, excited – but also completely comfortable.

Like he said, I felt I'd known him all my life.

He was still smiling at me impishly, his head slightly downward, his mouth half-cocked.

"So, I was wondering..." he began, his hand running through his thick mane again. "I was wondering if you'd be interested in having drinks with me sometime."

He wasn't looking me in the eye. Almost like he was shy. This guy, shy? He no doubt had women dripping all over him. Which almost made me turn him down. He had to be a womanizer. Anyhow, he was stratospheres out of my league. Light years. He was the Starship Enterprise, and I was Earth.

Or so went my brain. My heart, however, was noticing how comfortable I felt in his presence. Heart overruling brain, I simply said, "Sure."

He smiled. "Friday night at Harry's? We can meet for Happy Hour and go from there."

"Want to return to the scene of the crime, eh?" I asked with a smile.

"Something like that."

At that, we made a date to meet at Harry's at 5:30 on Friday.

After he left, Melinda said, "Oh, sweet Jesus, that guy is beautiful. Where did you find him?" She was mock-fanning herself as she talked.

I smiled. "You wouldn't want to know." *Your boss is a ho*. "Now, shoo, get back to work."

Friday couldn't get here fast enough.

Beautiful Illusions: Chapter Three

Friday was finally here. I couldn't quite believe this beautiful guy wanted to see me again, and it occurred to me, much to my acute embarrassment, that I didn't remember his name. I didn't know how to ask him about that.

I was in rare form, sleeping with a guy I'd just met and getting that schnockered in the first place. It had been at least since college since I'd done something like that, and have no memory of it the next day.

Maybe he slipped me a roofie? God, I hoped not. I wouldn't want to think a guy like that would be a rapist. Lord knew he wouldn't have to resort to that to bed a woman.

No, I got that wasted all on my own. That was what happened when I started tequila shots. The old shirt that said "One tequila, two tequila, three tequila, floor" summed up my reaction to that particular liquor. But somehow, I not only acted coherently but charmingly as well. Astounding.

That afternoon, I left the office early for a hair appointment and a Brazilian. Yowch! They should use Brazilians as a torture method for enemy combatants. That would get them talking in no time.

Not that I was planning on sleeping with the guy again that night. My sober self was much more old-fashioned than that.

Meeting him out, I was wearing my only pair of nice shoes, the red glitter Mary Jane Jimmy Choos from the night I met him. Those were my lucky shoes. They sure were lucky the other night, anyhow. They were high-heeled, but that was good because I needed the height. I stood 5'2", and this guy was at least 6'1".

I pulled on a slimming black dress with a halter neck, which was always my most flattering neckline. I felt self-conscious about my 30 extra pounds, then tried to banish the thought. A bit of foundation to cover up my freckles, some mascara for my light eyelashes, some lip gloss, and I was ready to go.

I got to the bar and looked around. Harry's was a classy upscale cigar bar where they served 30 different kinds of martinis, along with a limited menu mainly consisting of olives, hummus and different gourmet pizzas. It attracted an older crowd of sophisticates attracted to the expensive martinis and even more expensive cigars. The place was smallish, but it wasn't a hole in the wall, as it was two levels and had a patio. The interior walls were cherry wood, as was the enormous bar, which ran the length of the main room. The floor was covered in white tile. The artwork in this bar favored Toulouse Lautrec – brightly colored, with dancing girls and advertisements that looked like they were from the turn of the century. The crowd ranged from mid-20s to mid-60s, but most of the people in here were in their early thirties, by the looks of it.

Beautiful man was already there. I looked at him and

lost my breath momentarily. Dressed down in a blue short-sleeved shirt that brought out the marine flecks in his otherwise green eyes, with grey casual pants and black shoes, he looked like a Ralph Lauren model come to life. The short sleeves displayed his lean and muscular arms, and he looked like he didn't have an ounce of fat.

He stood up when he saw me, a broad smile on his face.

Now I was shaking. Not sure why I was having this reaction now. In my office, I felt much more comfortable. Maybe because it was my home turf. But here, in the bar, I felt intimidated.

I'd have to resist the urge to drink tonight. Alcohol was always my crutch in awkward social situations. Or any social situations. I was quite shy. Or insecure, at least.

He met me halfway and gave me a big hug. His body was warm and incredibly hard. He must've lived at the gym. I could hear his heart pounding as my head lay against his chest.

We sat down, and he ordered a Dewar's and water for him, a Grey Goose dirty martini for me.

So much for my vow not to drink tonight.

Well, I'll only have a few.

The drinks came shortly, and I knew I had to get the name issue out of the way.

"So," I began.

"Sorry, before you say anything, I just wanted to tell you that you look beautiful."

I momentarily forgot my words. I pondered anew the possibility that I was on some kind of candid camera and that my humiliation would soon be on YouTube. I then just managed to say, "Thank you."

"Now, you were saying," he said, looking at me with a soft expression.

I took a deep breath. "This is the most embarrassing thing I've ever had to admit. But I, well, you know, I had a lot to drink the other night and-"

"Ryan. My name is Ryan." He was still smiling, and his eyes told me he thought it was humorous that I forgot his name.

I could feel my face flushing. "How did you know what I was going to ask?"

He shrugged. "I figured that if you didn't remember me at all when I came into your office, it stands to reason you didn't remember my name, either."

"About that. I hope you don't think I make a habit of going home with men from a bar."

"Damn. I was hoping to get you hammered again and get you to pick up a girl and do a three-way," he said with a smile.

I laughed at that. "Sorry to burst your bubble," I said.

"Well, I understand you're embarrassed. But don't be. It was, uh, fun."

Fun. I wished I could've remembered.

"Anyhow, I could say the same," he said. "I hope you don't think I'm some kind of manwhore."

"No, no, I don't think that at all." I paused, tucking my hair behind my ear and sipping my drink. It was salty and slightly sour. As I picked one of the olives from the little red toothpick to put in my mouth, I saw Ryan watching me interestedly. "I also wanted to apologize for just, you know, leaving in the morning."

"Yeah, I was disappointed. I wanted to take you for breakfast."

"I was totally embarrassed for being there. It was shitty of me to do that, though."

"Well, I was glad you gave me one of your business

cards at the bar. Otherwise, I would have to do some serious research to find you." He took a sip of his scotch rocks. "And I would've tried to find you. Make no mistake about that."

Wow. I must've been really charming the other night. Or really "fun."

He was smiling. "I know we're doing this backward, but we need to get to know each other."

I couldn't remember what I told him, so I didn't know if he knew the basics about me. This was so awkward, not knowing if what I told him would be something he'd already heard.

"So, what do you know about me?" I asked him.

"That you're an attorney who aspires to do something else. Maybe become a writer or an animal rights activist. You want to eradicate all big money from politics and liberate every factory farm animal on the face of the earth. That you have gorgeous red hair."

Ryan crunched on some ice thoughtfully, then shook his now-empty glass and looked around for the waitress. She was there in a flash to take our next order. Then he continued. "And you think *The Importance of Being Earnest* was the funniest story you've ever read."

"Wow. I really was spouting off, wasn't I?" I knew that I tended not to have a filter when I was drinking, but I still couldn't believe I told this guy my life story in one sitting. And, of course, I was a hypocrite because, while I was a deep animal lover, I ate chicken and fish.

"No, not spouting off. You just came off as....passionate. You think about the world even though you know you can do little about it. That's refreshing. You're like a realistic idealist." He picked up a bar napkin, laid it down, and started doodling on it. The guy was quite an artist. Not looking up, he proceeded. "And the fact you said an Oscar Wilde play is one of your favorites really drew me in. Because he's one of my favorite playwrights too."

I blinked, not quite grasping what was going on. It all seemed surreal. As surreal as the drawing on the napkin was turning out. After it was done, he handed it to me with a smile. "For you," he said.

The drawing was a like a miniature Dali painting, with little melting hearts into fingertips and a single eye hovering above. It was charming, and I couldn't believe he put it together so quickly.

"Impressive," I began. "So, let me guess. You're a graphic artist?"

He shook his head. "Bank CEO."

"Ah. Should've known."

"Why is that?"

"You looked like a CEO the other day. All suited up."

He stirred his drink, squeezing his lime into it. His eyes didn't meet mine.

I instinctively knew something was wrong, so I asked him.

"Nothing's wrong. I just like you, that's all."

"I like you too," I said. But why did he seem to not want to talk to me about himself?

Grab your copy...
vinci-books.com/beautiful-illusions